Ghostly Waves

Lorna Shadow cozy ghost mystery - book 7

K.E. O'Connor

K.E. O'Connor Books

Chapter 1

I wrinkled my nose as I stared at the two options available. I couldn't believe I still had the leopard print thong given to me as a joke gift by Helen. It was a choice of the thong or the off-white giant granny knickers that should have been incinerated years ago.

Where had all my underwear gone since moving into our new house?

Shifting my phone to my other ear, I focused on my conversation with Josie, the agent at Prestige Recruitment Agency. "You said this new position is in Cornwall?"

"It sounds incredible," Josie twittered, her voice its usual two octaves too high. "And I thought you could do with somewhere lovely, given your last position didn't work out so well."

There was an awkward silence. I stared at my underwear and shook my head. "You mean with most of the family getting arrested?" My short-lived position working for the Cornells had been eventful and not one I wished to repeat.

"It was all so embarrassing," Josie said. "That'll teach me not to take a long holiday again. I'd never have let you stay there if I'd have been around. You're my favorite clients."

"We managed okay." I did a slow turn in my new duck egg blue bedroom. Maybe Zach had hidden my underwear? Did he have a secret liking for wearing my knickers when I wasn't around? I couldn't think of anyone less likely to enjoy dressing up in my underwear. He was a practical man through and through.

"And I know you were supposed to go back to the other position in Yorkshire," Josie said, "but the family decided to stay abroad. They won't be back for two years."

"I can't say I blame them," I said. "The castle they lived in is drafty. And I love Cornwall. this new position sounds great."

"And the Carlisles are super," Josie said. "You'll be working for Julianne Carlisle, but there'll be other administrative tasks. Helen will have the role of laundress, with full seamstress responsibilities. Also, the family runs a successful vineyard in the south-west. You could get the chance to sample the local wine. That would be a bonus." Josie was working hard on selling this job.

I smiled to myself. The position sounded good, lots of variety and in a beautiful part of the country so I could go exploring with Flipper on my days off.

Cornwall was full of intriguing coves and beaches and so many wild, diverse green spaces, I'd be spoilt for choice.

Helen and I deserved a break. After being chased around by scary mobster types in our last place and breaking our backs moving into our new house, this had come along at just the right time.

We'd only been in our gorgeous new home a few weeks, but I was tired of the smell of fresh paint and plaster. This position in Cornwall would get me away from the DIY and give us some much-needed income so we could furnish the house and make it a real home. I might also invest some of that money in new underwear if I couldn't find what I already owned.

"What do you reckon?" Josie asked. "I've forwarded your details to the family. They think you and Helen sound perfect."

"We'll take it," I said. "And they're fine with dogs?" I looked over to where Flipper was snoozing on the bottom of the bed, one gray paw tucked over his muzzle. Next to him lay Jessie, Zach's dog. She was curled on her side, a happy doggy grin on her face as one paw rested against Flipper. They never left each other's side. It was true love.

"They are," Josie said. "I never forget about Flipper. When I mentioned him to Julianne, she said they used to have dogs in the family, so it won't be any problem having him there."

"When do they need us to start?" I screwed up the leopard print thong and the granny pants and shoved them back in the drawer.

"They'd appreciate it if you could get there tonight."

"That shouldn't be a problem," I said. So long as I could find some decent underwear. I yanked open another drawer and rifled through it. Zach might have moved my things and had forgotten to tell me. I shoved aside a pair of his black socks. My hand hit a small jewelry box at the back of the drawer.

I pulled it out, and my jaw dropped. It looked like a ring box. I squeaked in surprise, and I never squeak.

"Are you still there?" Josie asked. "Is everything okay?"

"I'm not... well, yes, everything is fine with the job. Tell the family we'll be there tonight." I ended the call, and my hand shook as I placed down my phone. What was Zach doing with a ring box hidden in his sock drawer?

My heart thudding, I eased the box lid open.

"You have to hear the argument Helen is having with Gunner over him wanting to move his drum kit into the house." Zach walked into the room, a towel around his waist, fresh out of the shower and smelling of lime and lemon shower gel.

I spun around and hid the jewelry box behind my back, pulling my face into what I hoped was a mask of innocence.

He gave me a curious look. "Are you all right?"

"Everything's fine." My fingers curled around the box as guilt flashed through me. If Zach had bought this ring with a plan to propose, I shouldn't be snooping a peek.

"Has Josie found you and Helen new jobs?" He walked over to the king-sized bed, ruffling the dogs' furry heads as he passed them.

"Yep. Down in Cornwall."

He raised an eyebrow. "That's quite a journey."

"It is, but it sounds lovely." I tried to ease open Zach's sock drawer and place the ring box back without him noticing, but couldn't find the handle. "Six months in the Cornish sunshine. And the family owns a vineyard. I could send you back a few bottles of wine."

"I'd rather have you here." He grinned. "But I understand why you want to get away. Sorry I couldn't get the house finished before we all moved in."

The plan had been for Zach and Gunner to have everything installed, all the plastering and painting done, and then we'd pick the furniture before moving in, the four of us—me, Zach, Helen, and Zach's older brother, Gunner. But Zach had been offered an enticing horticultural job, and Gunner became tied up in cracking a big case, and the timeline slid. Fresh paint and cardboard boxes were our everyday surroundings.

"I don't mind," I said. "I'm just happy we're finally here. Although, it would be nice to sit on something sturdier than a rickety wooden chair and eat out of plastic containers." Zach and Gunner had worked as hard as they could to get the house ready, but without the money to finish it, we were still living in a building site.

"We can always come down for a long weekend," Zach said. "It's been years since I've been to Cornwall. I used to go there as a kid with the family, go rock pooling and seal watching. And the walking down there is great. There are loads of coastal paths to explore."

"I've always dreamed of retiring there," I said, "taking long walks along the beach and enjoying a few cream teas."

"I'll join you in that." Zach dropped his towel, giving me a wonderful view of his toned muscles before he shrugged into a pair of black combat trousers. As a gardener, Zach had a lean, toned body that came from hours of turning soil and digging holes. It was a look that suited him, and one I was always happy to leer at, as all good girlfriends should.

"It'll be good to have a break from all the work on the house," I said.

"What's the place like in Cornwall?" Zach pulled a green linen shirt from the closet and shrugged it on.

"You mean, how old is it? How many ghosts might be living there?" My ability to see ghosts was something I never put on my resume, but I often ended up using that particular skill, especially when working in old buildings. The older the house, the more ghosts there usually were.

"That's always of interest to me. I need to make sure you won't get yourself into too much trouble."

"As if I would." I grinned at him.

He gave me a frown, but it wasn't serious. "After your last job, you must want a break from all the ghost hunting."

"We cracked a huge case," I said. "Thanks to that ghost, Gunner's looking like the golden boy in the police. He solved a robbery no one else could."

"And he hasn't stopped bragging about it," Zach said, giving an exaggerated sigh. "If his head gets any bigger, it won't fit through the front door." He looked around the bedroom and scratched his chin.

"Are you missing something?"

"My watch," Zach said. "I left it in here before I took a shower."

I looked around. "I haven't seen it. You didn't leave it in the bathroom?"

"No. I always leave it on the nightstand."

"Since we're talking about missing things, you don't happen to know where all my underwear is?"

Zach raised his eyebrows. "In the laundry hamper?"

I scowled at him. "I do the washing regularly enough. And I'd do it more often if Helen didn't insist on taking over all the time. You know what she's like, obsessed with making sure everything is clean, has no holes in it or stains on it. I'm sure she checks the hamper every day."

"Well, I haven't moved your underwear."

"I only have two pairs of knickers left." I decided not to show Zach what my two options were.

"Maybe it's time you go shopping." He gave me a grin. "I could help you pick out something we'd both like."

"I don't need any more knickers," I said, feeling my cheeks warm. "I just need to find the underwear I already have."

"Are you sure you're looking in the right place?"

"Are you sure you are when it comes to your missing watch?"

Zach frowned. "Yes. I am. And while we're on the subject of missing things, what about my trainers?"

I crossed my arms over my chest. "What about them?"

"Have you put them somewhere?"

"What use would I have for your trainers? They're too big for me."

"I've always kept them under the bed," Zach said. "I went to get them out the other day, and they're gone."

"And you thought I'd taken them?"

He ran a hand through his damp hair. "I didn't say that. I just wondered if you'd put them somewhere else. Maybe you like to put things under the bed, and my trainers were getting in the way."

I forced down my irritation. We were both new to living together. Being in a relationship was all about compromise. I'd read that on a blog. "I haven't seen your trainers. Maybe the dogs took them."

"Jessie's never shown any interest in playing with my shoes," Zach said. "What about Flipper?"

At the sound of his name, Flipper raised his head and blinked his ice blue eyes at us.

"Flipper would never chew your trainers," I said.

"I didn't say he'd chew them." Zach said. "He could have played with them, took them outside, and they got lost in the garden."

"Have you looked in the garden?"

Zach let out a sigh. "Not yet. I'll go look now. Perhaps I'll find my watch out there, too." He strode out of the room and slammed the door behind him.

I resisted the urge to throw the ring box at him. As if Flipper or I would be interested in his smelly shoes.

I looked at Flipper, and he tilted his head to one side. "I bet he's put them in a closet somewhere and forgotten about it."

Flipper whined and looked at the ring box still in my hand.

I rested the tips of my fingers on the top of it, but no longer wanted to look inside. The thrill of finding it had faded. I placed the ring box back in Zach's sock drawer and closed it.

It suddenly felt like we had a long way to go before we'd be ready to take the next step in our relationship. If we fell out over something as silly as missing shoes and underwear, we couldn't hope to spend the next fifty years together in wedded bliss.

I took a deep breath. A little break from paint, missing things, and Helen's arguments with Gunner was what I needed. Cornwall would be perfect.

Chapter 2

Four hours later, Helen had driven us over halfway to our new job. Our suitcases were in the trunk and Flipper was fast asleep on the back seat of the car. The windows of Helen's bright red car were down and she was singing along to a pop tune on the radio.

I joined in, but was still distracted by my argument with Zach, turning over the possibilities of what had happened to our missing things. Why would Zach want to hide my knickers?

Helen flipped off the radio and tapped her fingers on the steering wheel, her blonde hair blowing in the breeze. "What's up with you?"

"Nothing a new set of underwear won't cure."

She shot me a curious glance. "What do you mean?"

"I'm not sure I mean anything. I only had two pairs of knickers left this morning, neither of them suitable."

"I do the laundry regularly. I'm sure I've missed none of your frillies."

"I don't think you have. And, just so you know, I don't expect you to do the laundry for us all."

Helen grinned. "I enjoy it. I did a load two days ago. You can't have run out already."

"I know I haven't," I said with a frustrated sigh. "This morning, it was only leopard skin thong or granny pant gray. And I got into a row with Zach over my underwear."

"Did you accuse him of stealing your knickers?"

"No! I asked if he'd moved them. Then he started going on about a missing watch and missing shoes and got all huffy with me and stormed out."

"Maybe Gunner borrowed his shoes. It would be the sort of thoughtless thing he'd do, take them without asking. He did that with the last muffin just the other day. And don't get me started on how he leaves the crusts on a sliced loaf and tells me there's plenty of bread left!"

I dragged my attention away from my knicker drama. "So, you and Gunner are still arguing?" Their relationship shot from one extreme to the other, with Helen either blushing furiously and batting her long, dark eyelashes or proclaiming her hatred for him.

"It's... complicated."

"And it will stay complicated until you talk to each other without fighting," I said. "We all live in the same house. You can't keep rowing. It makes the atmosphere tense."

"I wouldn't argue with him if he wasn't such a bull head."

"Are you sure you don't have a little bit of bull headedness in you, as well?"

"Not a drop." Helen scowled at me. "What were you saying about missing underwear?"

I grinned at her unsubtle change of topic. "Maybe I made a mistake. It feels like we've been unpacking boxes for weeks. I could have stuffed them in the wrong place and forgotten about it."

"It's possible. I found my eyelash curlers in the cutlery drawer last week. I was sure I had them on my vanity table. There they were when I went to get a strainer."

"It's good to know I'm not the only one going crazy and putting things in strange places."

"It's not craziness. We're busy working women. The men in our lives should be more considerate."

"Gunner is definitely in your life?"

She flashed me a nervous smile. "He has potential."

"Seriously! You're finally admitting you like him?" It was about time they got themselves sorted and either dated or stuck to the frenemy zone and went out with other people.

"I'm tolerating him," Helen said. "And he's not so bad to look at when he's not showing off or making out like he's some hotshot. He's got everyone he works with convinced he cracked the Cornell gold heist case. That was our doing. Well, you and the ghosts, but I assisted."

"He can hardly admit that he got helped by two amateurs and some ghosts. That would give him a one-way ticket to the unemployment line. I bet you wouldn't find him so attractive then."

"It's not his job that appeals to me."

"Why the sudden declaration of interest?"

Helen shrugged. "He's mentioned a colleague."

I raised my eyebrows. "A *female* colleague?"

"Matilda," Helen said, snitching her nose. "That sounds like the name for a heifer."

I laughed. "I'm sure she's a very nice lady."

"She probably is." Helen scowled.

"And you're worried Gunner will lose interest in you if Matilda is being lovely to him?"

"It's crossed my mind." Helen's fingers whitened as she gripped the steering wheel. "He reckons she's been baking him brownies. I should do that. No one can beat my brownies."

"He is into you," I said. "That won't change. And I'm sure he thinks your brownies are the best around. It could be that Gunner's mentioning Matilda because he wants to see if you get jealous, and it spurs you into action."

"It's working," she muttered.

"So, stop messing around with him and tell him how you feel."

"What if it doesn't work out?" she asked. "We're living together. If we get together and then fall out, it'll make things super awkward. Gunner is Zach's brother, so you'll feel bad for having to be mean to Gunner."

"I won't be mean to Gunner if things don't work out between you," I said.

"You should when he cheats on me with Matilda."

"You aren't even dating!" I shook my head. "And I could say the same for Zach and me. If he keeps accusing me of hiding his things, we could split up. That will be just as awkward."

"You're different," Helen said. "You've been together forever. You'll be getting married next."

Pressing my lips together, I looked out the window. I wasn't ready to confess to Helen what I'd discovered in Zach's sock drawer. I was still in shock. A ring box! It could only mean one thing. Were we ready to take that next step? Was I prepared to become Mrs. Zach Booth?

"You're not thrilled by the idea of marriage?" Helen asked.

"Maybe one day." I tapped my fingers against my knee. "Are you looking forward to spending a few months in Cornwall?"

"It's my favorite county." Helen grinned. "And I read through the particulars. The house has a sea view."

"And the family has a yacht," I said. "That's where we're meeting Marcus Patel, Julianne's assistant. He'll show us around the yacht, then take us to the family home."

"How exciting. I've always fancied myself on a yacht, sipping champagne and cruising around the Mediterranean while topping up my tan. That's what I should marry into. Not life as a worried policeman's wife, never knowing what my cheating, brownie eating husband is getting up to on his late shift with his female colleagues."

"Enough doom and gloom over your non-existent relationship with Gunner," I said. "Besides, if you were a yacht bunny, you'd get wrinkles. Doesn't that worry you?"

"I'd wear factor fifty sunscreen." She grinned. "You'd better keep a wetsuit on if you're going to be on deck in the sun. I don't think I've ever seen your skin with more than a couple of freckles."

Whereas Helen turned a beautiful golden brown as soon as the sun hit her, I was lucky if I got away with a freckle and peeling shoulders. No matter how hard I tried, I could never tan. I'd accepted my fate as pale and interesting, and did as Helen suggested and kept covered up in the sun. I didn't want to risk a bright pink nose and blistered skin.

"I don't know if we'll get the chance to do any cruising on the yacht, but I always enjoy seeing how the other half live." And that was the beauty of this job. We lived in some of the most incredible houses in the country and sampled delights we could never afford on our salaries.

We traveled for another hour before Helen left the main road, following the GPS directions as we drew closer to our destination.

As we crested the top of a hill, I let out a gasp. The sea was in front of us, the light sparkling off the waves and boats bobbing on the tide. As I looked down the hill, I spotted numerous pastel colored cottages and knew I was in Cornwall, a county of wild contrasts and often wonderfully eccentric people.

"It's five miles to go until we get to the harbor," Helen said.

Lowering my window, I sucked in deep breaths of the sea air, relaxing now we were almost there. I loved living with Zach and having a place to call home, but it was nice to get away.

I already missed Zach, though, and regretted our argument. It was silly to fight over knickers, watches, and shoes.

I craned my neck as the marina came into view. The sun dazzled as it reflected off the glass and chrome of the yachts moored in the marina. They ranged in size from small day skippers to fast, luxury yachts oozing with ostentatious wealth.

We parked in the Ocean Pleasures Marina car park, and I was glad to get out and stretch my legs. I'd seen enough of the inside of Helen's car.

"Which boat is ours?" Helen shielded her eyes with her hand and looked around.

"It's called the Orwell. It was named after the science-fiction writer, George Orwell." I let Flipper out the back seat of the car.

He stretched before looking around his new environment with interest.

"I hope it's one of the big ones," Helen said. "I'm not good with small boats."

"I didn't know you get seasick. We've been on boats before and you were always fine."

"It has been known. I'm fine on big boats."

"Let's find you a big boat then." I hooked my arm through her elbow, and we waked along the marina, checking out the names of the moored boats. Lots of them had women's names, such as *Desdemona* and *Josephine*. Named after wives or mistresses, most likely.

"This is it." Helen hurried forward, while I tugged Flipper away from sniffing a pair of flip-flops left on the jetty.

We stopped by an enormous white yacht. It must measure twenty meters, with a raised pilothouse, upper and lower California deck, and fishing cockpit. It rocked gently on the water as we stared at it.

"Wow! This is quite something," Helen said.

"Big enough for you?" I asked.

A man stepped out from below deck, a bucket of champagne in one hand and three glasses in the other. He wore a cream linen suit without a wrinkle on it, a red shirt underneath, and deck shoes with no socks. His skin was chocolate brown and his black hair immaculately gelled into place.

He turned toward us and smiled. "Are you Lorna and Helen?"

"That's right," I said. "Are you Marcus?"

"I am. Come aboard. You're most welcome." Marcus placed the champagne and glasses on the table on the deck. "I'm Julianne's assistant. Her right-hand man, if you like." He hurried over and held out his hand as we both climbed aboard.

"Thanks." I noticed the smoothness of Marcus's hand. He looked like he'd just had a manicure. He put my nails to shame.

"Welcome to the Orwell." Marcus's voice was warm and devoid of any accent.

"It's a lovely boat," Helen said as she looked around.

Marcus grimaced. "It is. Better not call it a boat around here or they'll throw you out of the marina. The technical term is a yacht. Not that I know much about the yacht, just so long as it goes and there are no holes in it." He laughed politely at his own joke.

"Does the family use the *yacht* a lot?" I asked Marcus.

"Not so much. Julianne's husband was a real fan of the water."

"He doesn't get out much?"

Marcus adjusted the cuff of his jacket. "Not so much. Would you both like a glass of champagne? Julianne told me to take the best of care of you both and to show you around and make you comfortable."

"That would be lovely." Helen gave him a bright smile as she continued her inspection of the Orwell.

Marcus made swift work of opening the champagne, and we were soon sipping bubbles and enjoying the view as he told us about the area and the jet-set crowd he mingled with.

"This yacht isn't the best here, but it's up there with some of the lovely ones. It's got a long-range motor, twin CAT engines, and a wave runner. Perfect if you fancy a week in Mexico sea fishing," he said.

So much for him not knowing anything about yachts. "Like you said, so long as it doesn't have any holes, I'm happy."

"Julianne likes to come here and work on board," Marcus said, not picking up on my sarcasm. "She calls it her second office. She rarely takes the yacht out, but likes the view and to get away from the house, sometimes."

"I'm fine with working on board a yacht," I said.

"It's fully equipped. Let me show you down below." He led us below deck and presented a luxurious lounge decked out in muted gray and cream. There were also three bedrooms, along with the bathroom and kitchen. It was all tasteful and expensive looking. "You'd barely know you were on the water if it weren't for the rocking sensation."

"It is rather vigorous, isn't it?" Helen placed a hand on her stomach.

"Are you feeling okay?" Her cheeks looked worryingly pale.

"I just need some fresh air." Helen thrust her champagne flute at me and dashed up the steps, leaving Flipper and me with Marcus.

His gaze went to Flipper, who'd been following us around as we made the tour. "Does he go everywhere with you?"

"He has to," I said. "He's my assistance dog. Flipper helps me with a medical condition."

Marcus's immaculate dark eyebrows rose. "Nothing serious?"

"Nothing that Flipper and I can't handle." Flipper's ghost hunting skills were much better than mine. That was when he wasn't distracted by a fox or a cat or anything else on four legs. Or food. He came in handy when there was a ghost around. He was my furry ghost detector.

"Well, may I say you look far too radiant to be unwell." Marcus smiled. "I have a feeling both you and Helen will be popular at the yacht club."

"I'm not sure we'll get time for socializing," I said, not liking the idea of being paraded around the club like a trophy.

"Julianne's a generous employer and likes to make life comfortable for everyone," Marcus said. "And, as you know, accommodation is provided as part of your contract. I have a room on the top floor of the house. It has one of the best views. Perhaps I can show you."

"I'm sure the view from my window will be pretty enough."

Marcus gave a small sniff. "Anyway, you'll get plenty of time off if you want to come to the club with me as a guest. Julianne doesn't spend a lot of time at the house. Providing you get the work done, your time is your own."

"That seems fair." More than fair, she sounded like the perfect boss. But I wouldn't use my spare time going to the yacht club on Marcus's arm anytime soon.

"There are always eligible bachelors at the yacht club," Marcus said. He tilted his head and lowered his eyelids. "That's if you're looking."

"I'm definitely not looking." I decided to shut Marcus down before he went any further. "I'm happily living with my boyfriend."

He nodded. "I'm not surprised to hear that. He's a very lucky man."

I smiled at him. "I think so."

"And Helen?" Marcus twirled his empty glass between his fingers.

"It's complicated. I'll let her explain things to you."

He sighed. "It often is with beautiful women."

"Are you married?"

"Only to my job," Marcus said, his gaze flitting around the lounge. "I have ambitions to own a yacht like this one day. I'm learning everything I can from the Carlisles so I can grow my empire. In five years' time, I'll have all of this and more."

Flipper's ears pricked up and he hurried to the other side of the lounge. He jumped up and put his paws on the window ledge to peer out onto the deck.

"Is someone coming?" I followed Flipper and looked out the window, but couldn't see anybody.

Flipper jumped down from the window and circled the room, his gaze intent as if he was seeking something.

I looked around, but couldn't get any sense of a ghostly presence. No cold spells, no light-headedness, no chills, just a slight buzz from the expensive champagne.

"Is something wrong with your dog?" Marcus watched Flipper hunting around.

"Maybe he doesn't like being below deck," I said. "He's not been on many yachts." I did another discreet check of the room, but couldn't see anything that would unsettle him.

"Let's go back on deck," Marcus said. "You've seen everything down here. I'll show you around the marina and then take you to the house and you can meet the family."

Flipper stayed close to my side as we headed back on deck, but kept glancing over his shoulder as if something was following him.

His behavior set me on edge. Goose bumps prickled across my arms, but I saw nothing to suggest there was a ghost around. It could simply be the motion of the waves making Flipper feel strange.

As we got on deck, I spotted Helen at the other end of the yacht, leaning over the side and taking in deep gulps of air, her hands gripping the railing.

I walked over and stopped by her side. "Feeling any better?"

"I think I need to be on a bigger boat," she whispered. "I'm just glad I don't have to work on this thing like you'll have to."

"Boats have never bothered me," I said. "And there won't be any need for you to come on here and do the laundry. You'll be safe at the house until you get your sea legs."

Helen gave quick nod. "Any chance we can get off this thing?"

"Oh dear." Marcus hurried to the side of the yacht and looked toward the marina car park.

"Is something wrong?" I asked.

"This isn't on the schedule. Julianne is here. And she's with Honey."

Chapter 3

Marcus paced back and forth, wringing his hands together. "I didn't expect her here today. I had it all planned. I was to show you around and then take you to the house. Julianne should stick to the schedules I give her."

"It's not a problem Julianne's here, is it?" I asked.

"No, of course not. This is her yacht. Julianne can come and go as she chooses. But I like to have things laid out for when she arrives. Nothing is ready." He turned toward the door to go below deck, but stopped and turned back, his hands fluttering in the air.

"I'm sure she'll be fine."

"You don't understand. Julianne is never fine when she's with Honey."

"Who's Honey?" Helen asked.

"A work experience girl," Marcus said. "She's sweet enough. Although, I don't know what Blake was doing taking her on, especially with me here. She has no experience."

"Perhaps that's why he took her on," I said. "We all have to start somewhere."

"She's not cut out for this kind of work," Marcus said. "I haven't got a clue what her background is. It's not in business."

"So long as Mr. Carlisle is happy with her, that's the main thing."

Marcus shot me a glare. "Come on, you'd better meet Julianne."

I raised my eyebrows at Helen as we followed Marcus and waited by the side of the yacht for Julianne and Honey to arrive. Marcus enjoyed controlling things around here.

As Honey grew closer, I got an idea why Blake might have hired her. She was stunning, with enormous blue eyes, curves that put Helen's to shame, and a mane of blonde hair, the roots peeking through showing she wasn't a natural blonde. Somehow, that made her even more attractive and gave her a sultry air.

Julianne strode along, ahead of Honey, her hands clasped in front of her. She was also an attractive woman in her mid-thirties, wearing a fitted flowered dress, her hair strawberry blonde. She had the classic good looks of most wealthy people, her makeup expertly applied and her hair blow dried.

"Try not to notice that Julianne and Honey aren't friendly with each other," Marcus muttered. "They have trouble getting along."

As if on cue, Julianne slowed and glared at Honey. "This will be the last time I tell you, you're not to go into his study."

"I was looking for a map," Honey said, her voice so low I could barely hear her. "Blake wouldn't have minded me looking."

"You have no clue what my husband would like," Julianne snapped. Her gaze shot to Helen and me and her eyes narrowed.

Marcus hurried off the yacht. "Julianne, I'd like you to meet Lorna Shadow and Helen Holiday." He extended his hand toward her, but she ignored him, her attention on us.

"I thought you were coming to the house?"

"We would have done," I said, "but Marcus asked as to meet him here to show us around the yacht."

Julianne's narrowed gaze shifted to Marcus. "Is Mr. Patel your employer?"

I gulped. "No, Mrs. Carlisle. I was simply following the instructions sent." This wasn't a good start to our working relationship.

"You received the wrong instructions." Julianne stepped onto the yacht and gave us both a brief handshake. "Marcus should not have changed the arrangements without checking with me first."

Marcus blinked rapidly. "I was only trying to be helpful. I know how busy you are."

"I'm never too busy to meet new members of the team." The sharpness in her voice vanished. "And call me Julianne. Mrs. Carlisle makes me sound ancient. I guess you've already had the tour, thanks to Marcus."

"I was just showing them around." Marcus wrung his hands together, his tone mournful.

"It's done now." Julianne waved a hand in the air. She smiled at us and her features softened. "I hope you find the yacht to your liking."

"It's lovely," I said.

"You can really feel the pull of the waves." Helen still looked pale.

"It's a peaceful place," Julianne said. "I like to get away from the house now and again and get work done on here without being disturbed."

"I'm happy to work wherever you need me to," I said.

"Is it okay if I come on board?" Honey still stood on the jetty.

"If you must." The smile slid from Julianne's face. "Just stay out of the way."

I extended a hand to Honey as she came on board. She shot a nervous glance at Julianne before shaking it. "It's nice to meet you."

"You too," Honey said.

"Pay her no attention," Julianne said. "She's my husband's work experience girl. She won't be here much longer."

Honey ducked her head, and her jaw clenched.

"If you want any tips about the work I do, you're welcome to them," I said quietly. "When I was first starting out, I didn't have a clue what I was doing."

"That's nice of you," Honey said.

"Honey's not cut out for your kind of work," Julianne said. "She'll be moving on soon."

Honey's hands clenched into fists, but she didn't respond.

Marcus cleared his throat. "I was going to show the ladies around the marina and take them for dinner in the yacht club."

"Another time," Julianne said. "We'll have dinner at the house. It's all arranged, unless you have also changed those plans without informing me."

Marcus gave a stiff bow. "Of course not. As you wish."

Julianne turned to step off the yacht and froze. "What's he doing here?"

I looked over to see a man heading unsteadily toward the yacht. He wore an open-necked white shirt and dark jeans. In one hand was a bottle of beer.

"I meant to let you know that Mr. Carlisle would be arriving today," Marcus said. "He'll be staying the week."

"Yes, you should have let me know," Julianne said irritably. "And he looks drunk, as usual."

"Is that your husband?" I asked.

"No, he most certainly isn't," Julianne said. "That's Channing. Blake's younger brother."

As Channing neared, I spotted several days' worth of stubble on his chin as he pushed his dark hair off his face. He flashed Julianne a smile and his blue eyes gleamed. "I thought I'd come and meet the new girls." He grinned at Helen and me.

"Get yourself sober before you bother them," Julianne said. "When you're in a fit enough state, you may join us for dinner."

"My state is just perfect." He leaped onto the yacht, stumbling forward and straight into Helen.

She gave a squeak of alarm as the sway of the Orwell made her off-balance and she pitched over. Channing landed on top of her with a surprised grunt.

"Leave Helen alone!" Julianne grabbed Channing's arm and tried to pull him up. "I must apologize for my brother-in-law."

"I'm terribly sorry." Channing smiled down at Helen, ignoring all attempts Julianne made at getting him to stand.

"No harm done." Helen shot me a pleading look. "If there's any chance I can get up, I'd appreciate it."

Channing laughed before hauling himself onto his knees, beer bottle still in one hand. "I have literally fallen for you. Well, fallen on top of you. It was rather fun."

Helen gave an embarrassed laugh as she stood and smoothed her dress down.

Julianne tutted and shook her head. "Why don't you go pester Honey, instead?"

Channing's eyebrows rose. "Isn't she working?"

"She's not doing anything important," Julianne said.

"Only because you won't let me," Honey muttered under her breath.

Julianne turned slowly. "What was that?"

"Nothing!" Honey said swiftly. "Channing, why don't I take you for a coffee?"

"You are a dear girl," he said. "I always knew Blake did the right thing by hiring you."

"You know nothing about it," Julianne said. "The two of you get off this yacht."

"I did nothing wrong," Honey said.

"You still being here is wrong."

Honey's mouth opened, but she clamped it shut, her lips pressed together and her head bowed. She turned and climbed off the yacht without another word, Channing ambling along behind her.

"If it weren't for that ridiculous employment contract my husband had drawn up, that girl would already be gone," Julianne said. "I only keep her on so she can't sue me for breach of contract."

I watched Honey go with interest. Julianne had made it clear she hated her, but I couldn't figure out why, unless her relationship with Blake was more than a professional one. When I got a moment alone with Honey, I'd see if she could clear things up.

Marcus cleared his throat again and shot a knowing look at Helen and me.

"You must excuse me," Julianne said as she turned toward us. "My husband's brother can be somewhat challenging. He's too fond of living the high life without having the money to afford it. He thinks he can dip into what isn't his. And as for Honey..." Her words trailed off as she watched Honey and Channing walk away.

"Families can be tricky," I said.

"That they can." Julianne placed her hands on the rail. "Let's go to the house. I'm sure you'd both like to freshen up and explore your new home."

"That sounds great," I said.

Flipper ran toward me, sat at my feet, and threw up.

Chapter 4

Mortification shot through me as I looked at the mess Flipper had vomited across the deck of the Orwell. "I'm so sorry." I looked around for something to clear the mess up with. "He's never normally ill."

Julianne raised her eyebrows. "That's not a problem. Marcus, you deal with this little accident. I'll accompany the girls back to the house."

Marcus looked horrified as he stared at the dog vomit marring the teak decking.

I muttered an apology as we hurried away. I kept my fingers wrapped around Flipper's collar and a close watch on him, just in case he decided on a repeat performance.

"It could be the motion of the yacht that made him unwell," Julianne said as she led us along the jetty back to the marina car park. "It gets us all, sometimes. It took me months to get comfortable on the yacht, so you have nothing to apologize for. Your dog must be feeling most unwell." She gave Flipper's head a quick pat.

I looked back to see Marcus holding a broom and furiously sweeping the deck. Julianne had seemed delighted at giving him the task of vomit cleaner.

"I came by cab," Julianne said as we reached Helen's car. "We'll take your car to the house."

"I'll sit in the back with Flipper and make sure he's okay. You take the front seat," I said to Julianne.

We all hopped in. I wrapped an arm around Flipper, giving him a quick check over to make sure everything seemed okay. Now he was off the yacht, he was back to his normal self, peering out the window as we shot along the narrow lanes toward the house.

"I won't be around much over the next couple of weeks," Julianne said. "I'm needed in London to take care of business. I'll leave you plenty of work and we can keep in touch via the telephone. And you always have Marcus to help out if you have questions. He has an answer for everything."

"He seems to have a good handle on things here," I said.

"Young Marcus has aspirations above his station, but I admire his ambition." Julianne had a thin smile on her lips.

"And Honey can always help me out."

Julianne scowled out the window. "That young woman will be gone soon. Don't come to rely on her for anything."

"She's not working out?" Helen shot me a look in the rear-view mirror.

"That's correct," Julianne said.

An uncomfortable silence slid around us. Clearly, there was a problem between Honey and Julianne.

"Will your husband be around?" I asked.

"I can guarantee that he won't," Julianne said. "Turn right up here and go through the back streets. That way, you'll avoid the tourists. They clog the narrow streets this time of year and can make it hellish to drive through."

Helen did as instructed, weaving her car around some extraordinarily tight bends. I kept my eyes closed as we shot along a cliff top road, praying Helen didn't get distracted and go all *Thelma and Louise* and shoot us over the edge.

"The next left is the house driveway," Julianne said, seeming unfazed by Helen's speedway style driving.

I let out a breath I didn't realize I'd been holding and relaxed my grip on the door handle as Helen drove through an open wooden gateway.

The house in front of me sat on a small rise, detached from any other properties. It had two stories and a gray slate roof. Neat rows of flowers sat under the ground floor windows and a gravel driveway led to the red front door.

There was a white van parked by the entrance, with a large silhouette of a dog on the side.

"It might not be much from the outside," Julianne said as she climbed out the car, "but it's beautiful inside. And from the back of the house, you have unspoiled views across the ocean. I can sit in a chair and stare at that view all day."

"It looks lovely." I got out with Flipper and walked around to take our cases out of the trunk.

"I like it," Julianne said. "My office overlooks the sea, so make sure you don't get too distracted by the views." She gave me a warm smile.

"I'm always a sucker for a good ocean view."

Her smile remained. She seemed relaxed now she was home. "This way. I'll show you to your rooms and let you settle in. I don't expect either of you to start work until tomorrow afternoon. I'll be up and out first thing, so take your time getting used to the house and figuring out where everything is."

This job was sounding better by the second. We followed Julianne through the front door and into a white painted open hallway. There was a set of stairs to the right-hand side and a long airy corridor leading to the rest of the house.

Julianne led us up the stairs and along a corridor, stopping by a door. She pushed it open to reveal a pale blue room, with one wall papered in colorful birds. There was a large double bed, a vanity unit, and a closet.

"I hope this is suitable," Julianne said, looking at me.

"Yes! It looks perfect."

"Helen, you're next door. You have a shared bathroom between the two of you."

I suppressed a frown. Helen took ages in the bathroom. I'd be the one rushing in after her, having to endure a cold shower and no chance to do my hair.

"You can use the kitchen whenever you like," Julianne said. "We're pretty relaxed about meals. Sometimes I dine alone. Other times, I have company. We cook for ourselves, but I have food delivered, so help yourselves to whatever you like. I've ordered in something special for us all tonight."

"We'll look forward to that," I said.

"I'll leave you both to settle in," Julianne said. "You must excuse me. I've got Taylor downstairs. I'm hoping she can find me a new dog. She did wonders with our old one. I miss not having a dog in the house. Join me later. We'll eat in an hour, and everyone will be there. You can get to know us all, and give you a chance to decide if we're too awful to work for."

I gave her my warmest smile. I sensed a sadness about Julianne. There was something going on behind her smile that I couldn't figure out. "I'm sure we'll both enjoy our time here."

"I hope you do." She gave us a nod goodbye before leaving.

As I walked into the room, I saw Flipper had settled himself on the foot of my bed and closed his eyes. That dog could sleep anywhere.

"Do you think Flipper's okay?" I stroked his head. I hated when he was unwell.

"He was just seasick, like me," Helen said. She did a quick circuit around the room before checking out her bedroom, coming back a moment later. "At least I kept my lunch down."

"He seemed anxious when we were on the yacht," I said.

"As in ghost seeing anxious?"

"I thought so, but I had a good nose around when we were below deck and couldn't sense anything strange. Maybe he just doesn't like being on the water."

"You'll have to leave him behind with me if you go work on the yacht with Julianne."

"He won't mind that, so long as he has a comfortable place to sleep. And I know you sneak him treats when I'm not looking." I petted his head and then unzipped my suitcase.

"Of course I do. He's my favorite dog." Helen sank onto my bed. "I can't say I'm unhappy about there being no ghosts on the Orwell. A nice normal job, with just your usual family dramas, wouldn't that be nice?"

I looked at Flipper again, and although his eyes were closed, his ears were alert, swiveling backward and forward as if trying to detect something. "Let's hope so. I'm sure everything will be fine, once he's settled in here."

"Maybe the sea air has tired him out."

I nodded as I continued to unpack. "I wonder if Mr. Carlisle will be at dinner. Julianne didn't seem keen on talking about him."

"And his brother, Channing," Helen said. "I'm sure I'll get a bruise on my backside from where he landed on top of me."

"It wasn't the most graceful of introductions. Fo you think Julianne will allow Honey at the table? She clearly doesn't like her."

"What's up with that?" Helen dangled her feet over the edge of my bed. "Honey seemed nice enough. Every time she opened her mouth, Julianne bit her head off."

"Perhaps she thinks her husband is up to no good with Honey."

"Not another cheater," Helen said with a groan. "We've had enough of those. Why can't we find a nice, happily married couple, who never argues or cheats on each other?"

"Because we live in the real world." I held up my only pair of knickers. I'd gone with the leopard print thong when getting dressed this morning and was regretting my choice. I'd forgotten how much thongs chaffed. "And tomorrow, we need to go underwear shopping."

"Why don't you send Marcus out to get you some?" Helen grinned. "I bet he can turn his hand to anything, running the family business, cleaning up dog puke. I'm sure knicker shopping isn't beneath him."

"I feel sorry for Marcus. There's no harm in being ambitious. Julianne was mean for making him clear that up."

"He came across as too keen," Helen said. "Julianne is showing him who's the boss."

"He was quick enough to check out if we were single."

Helen sat up. "What did you tell him about me?"

"That you're complicated."

"I'm not complicated," she said. "My situation is just a bit... tricky."

"I'll let Gunner know you think he's tricky."

"Not him." Helen scowled. "Our whole situation. Us all living together, him being such a big head, me not knowing if life as a policeman's wife is for me."

"You've discussed marriage?"

"Not for a second." She flung a pillow at me. "I like to plan things. It's always good to have a plan."

"Does Gunner realize he's included in this plan?"

"What he doesn't know won't hurt him," Helen said. "Besides, I've yet to make my mind up about him."

"Don't take too long," I said, "or Matilda might step into the slot with her sweet smiles and her brownies. You'll lose your chance."

"I'd like to see her try," Helen grumbled. "I'm going to unpack." She grabbed her case and flounced out of the room.

I grinned as she slammed the door. As I continued unpacking, I heard voices through the open window and walked over to see Julianne talking to a woman with a mass of dark curls. That must be Taylor. She had a large gray husky by her side, who hopped in the back of the van before Taylor waved and drove off.

I hung my clothes and sorted through my cosmetics and toiletries before selecting a smart black dress for dinner.

The long drive and the sea air had me yawning. I curled up next to Flipper on the bed. "How you doing, boy?"

He opened one eye, gave my nose a sniff, and then closed his eye.

"At least you've got no ghosts to worry about here. Everything seems nice and normal."

Flipper grumbled and covered his nose with a paw.

"I feel the same." I closed my eyes and snuggled against him. A five minute nap was just what I needed.

Clutching the side of the yacht, my stomach flipped as freezing icy water stung my eyes. The yacht bucked under my feet and a wave crashed over me, threatening to send me overboard.

Terror flooded my veins as the yacht rocked and more water poured across the deck. All around me was the sound of angry, hissing waves. As my terrified gaze shot around, all I could see was blackness. There was no light. I was alone on a ship that was about to capsize.

I took a deep breath and was about to scream for help, when another wave slammed into me and my mouth filled with salty, cold water. I coughed, spitting most of it out and hooked my elbow around the rail, determined not to go into the waves. Once I hit the water, that would be it. I'd be dead in seconds.

My nose itched, but I had to resist the urge to rub it, in case I lost my grip and tipped overboard. The itching intensified.

My eyes shot open to discover Flipper licking the end of my nose, concern in his eyes.

Letting out a relieved sigh, I gently pushed him away. It was a dream. "Thanks for waking me up. I was about to go for a swim."

I stood, washed the dog lick off my nose, changed into my evening dress, and we went to find Helen.

I rapped on her bedroom door, and she opened it. She wore a stunning cherry red dress and matching lipstick.

"Are you looking to impress someone tonight?" I asked.

"I wanted to make an effort." She looked at my hair and shook her head. "Have you been asleep?"

"For a few minutes. I wish I hadn't bothered. I had a horrible nightmare about being on board a yacht in a storm."

"It looks like you've been in an actual storm." Helen shut her bedroom door. "One side of your hair is flat and the other side looks like you've been electrocuted."

I attempted to neaten my hair with my hands. "Come on, there's no time to worry about my hair. Let's see what this family is really like."

Chapter 5

We headed down the carpeted staircase, the walls covered in dramatic landscape oil paintings, and stopped outside the dining room door.

Helen fussed with my hair before shaking her head. "You'll have to do."

"Thanks, Mom."

We walked into the dining room to find Julianne with Marcus standing next to her, and Honey in the corner on her own.

Channing was by the drinks cabinet, looking like he hadn't slowed down since we'd met that afternoon. He raised his glass when he spotted us. "Ladies, might I get you both a drink?"

Julianne glanced over at him and shook her head before smiling at us. "Welcome. And help yourselves to drinks. Ignore Channing's attempts to get you drunk."

"There's nothing wrong with having a few drinks. What will it be?" He waved a bottle of champagne in the air.

"Just a small one," I said.

"Ooooh! I love champagne." Helen grinned before hurrying over and taking two full glasses of bubbly from Channing.

"I am sorry for our unexpected introduction today," Channing said, giving Helen a lopsided smile. "I've never fallen for a girl so easily before. But you are jolly pretty."

"No harm done," Helen said as a blush crept across her cheeks.

"Didn't you mention something about a bruise?" I asked her, trying to look as innocent as possible.

"Don't say I hurt you?" Channing looked mortified. "You'll have to let me rub it better."

"No need." Helen's hand brushed across her backside. "And you didn't hurt me. Lorna's talking nonsense."

"You must let me make it up to you," Channing said. "I can show you around the village. Show you all the good spots, the places the tourists aren't aware of."

"You only know good places to go drinking," Julianne said from across the room.

"Naturally," Channing said, giving Helen a wink. "But there are some excellent restaurants around here, especially if you like seafood."

"It's one of my favorites," Helen said.

"Then it's a date." He leaned down and patted Flipper's head. "And your wolf dog can come along. Most of the local places are happy to accept well-behaved animals. Although I did hear an amusing rumor that this furry old fella lost his lunch on the Orwell. That's not a habit, is it?"

"No! That was a one-off." At least I hoped it was. If Flipper kept being sick, I'd have to take him to his least favorite place, the vet.

"Jolly good," Channing said. "Well, bottoms up and welcome to the family."

I looked around the room and noticed several oil paintings of what must be family members hanging on the walls. On the sideboard by the drinks cabinet was a picture of Julianne and what must be her husband, standing in a formal pose, both smiling at the camera. "Is this Mr. Carlisle?"

Channing nodded. "My brother."

"Will he be joining us tonight?"

Channing scratched his head. "Erm... that might be a problem."

"Is he away on business?" Helen asked.

Channing looked at the ground. "Ah, well, you see—"

"Dinner is served." Julianne gestured us toward the smartly laid wooden table. "Everyone take a seat. We've got crab tonight as a main course."

Channing gestured to the table. "Off you go, ladies. Julianne doesn't like to be kept waiting." He refilled his glass and took a large sip.

I wanted to know more about the elusive Mr. Carlisle, but it looked like Channing wasn't willing to share.

We walked over and took our seats. I could already smell a rich butter and parsley sauce drifting from the silver tureens in the center of the table. I was surprised to see Honey serving the dinner, hurrying around with a scowl on her face as she laid out the rest of the serving dishes.

Channing wandered around, filling everyone's glasses with white wine before taking his seat next to Helen, a glass of whiskey in one hand to accompany his own wine.

"This all looks lovely." Helen heaped vegetables and potatoes onto her plate.

"Most of the produce is local," Julianne said. "We like to support local businesses. We have many restaurants who take our wine, so we feel it's right to return the favor. These crabs were caught fresh today. Best you'll ever have."

I glanced at the empty seat at the head of the table. There was no place setting. "Is your husband joining us?"

Julianne glanced around the table as she flapped her napkin onto her lap. "He's not here."

Channing's eyebrows raised. "You haven't told them?"

A sense of unease curled around my spine, and Helen nudged my knee.

"Not yet," Julianne said, her gaze turning icy as she glared at Channing. "I didn't want to unsettle our new employees with sad news on their first day."

"Is there a problem?" I asked. "I hope Mr. Carlisle isn't ill."

"Not as such." Julianne played with her napkin. "It's simply that my husband, Blake, he passed away recently."

Helen kicked me under the table, and I repressed a grimace. "I'm sorry to hear that."

"It was a shock for us all," Julianne said. "I'm still not used to him being gone."

Honey dropped a serving spoon on the floor and rushed to pick it up.

"You're so clumsy," Julianne snapped. "That's everyone. You can leave now. We'll serve ourselves if we need any more."

"Sorry, Mrs. Carlisle." Honey dashed out of the dining room.

"That girl is hopeless," Julianne said. She turned back to us and let out a sigh. "Yes, poor Blake. It was a tragic accident. He loved that yacht. I imagine he felt safe there. He never expected to die on it."

"He died on the Orwell?"

"That's right," Channing said. "Poor guy fell overboard and drowned."

"So you say."

I jumped at the sound of a deep male voice behind me and turned to see a middle-aged man with a paunch, dressed in a dark suit, leaning against the doorjamb.

"James! I didn't expect you until tomorrow," Julianne said.

He sauntered into the room and gestured to the empty seat at the head of the table. "May I?"

"No one else will sit there," Julianne said with another sigh. "Grab a plate from the side and join us. There's plenty of food. You're so early. Your room isn't made up."

"That's not a problem. I know how to put a sheet on a bed. I got an earlier train. I've got a busy few days ahead of me." He looked around the table, his gaze stopping at Helen and me. "We've not met before. I'm James Pagent."

Julianne made the introductions. "This is their first day here. Lorna and Helen are just getting to know us."

James had a well-proportioned face, some might say handsome, with a strong jawline and bright blue eyes. His nose had a hint of someone who enjoyed too much wine, with tiny broken veins on the surface.

"What were you saying?" I asked James, keen to hear his theory about Blake's death. "You don't think Mr. Carlisle's death was an accident?"

"He was the best sailor around." James accepted wine from Channing and sat down. "Blake loved that yacht and could walk around it blindfolded. How he managed to fall overboard from the top deck when it was in the harbor makes no sense."

"The police investigated and said it was a tragic accident," Julianne said. "He got disorientated in the dark."

"He'd probably been drinking," Channing said. "That can make anyone unsteady on their feet."

"He could hold his alcohol." James drained half his wine glass. "Blake didn't fall."

"What are you suggesting?" Julianne asked. "Nobody would want to push my husband overboard. He was a good man."

"Yes, he was the best of men," James said. "I miss him not being around."

"Now he's not here, you must want control of the vineyard," Channing said.

"Not a chance! I leave all that to Julianne. This is a family business. I'd much prefer it if my oldest friend were still here overseeing things." James frowned at Channing. "My interest isn't in running a business."

"No, you just like drinking the profits," Channing said sharply.

James's gaze drifted to Channing's empty wine glass. "As do you."

I glanced over at Flipper, who sat patiently in the corner of the room, his eyes drifting from plate to plate as he looked at the delicious food. It made sense now why he was unwell on the yacht. He must have sensed Blake's presence and it made him feel bad. That was unusual. It was the first time he'd ever been sick when encountering a ghost.

"Losing Blake was the main reason I employed extra staff," Julianne said, turning her attention to me. "Blake did the finances, and I focused on the admin. I can't do it all on my own."

"I said I'd be more than happy to step up," Marcus said. He been quiet until now. "You only have to ask."

"You're still learning the ropes," Julianne said. "And when I read Lorna's resume, I knew she was the woman for this job."

"I won't let you down," I said. "Your business is in safe hands with me."

Marcus grumbled something under his breath before stabbing at his crab with a fork.

I'd need to be careful around Marcus. From the way he was attacking his food, he was not happy. I'd taken on the role he coveted.

I studied him out of the corner of my eye as he demolished his crab. Just how ambitious was Marcus? Perhaps he thought if he got rid of Blake, he'd be able to step into his shoes. It would be a great motive for murder.

"I can't help but feel a little guilty about what happened to Blake," James said. "We'd been out earlier that day and had a few drinks. I left him when he said he wanted time to himself. I offered to stay with him, but he said he had things to work out on his own."

"You've said this before," Julianne said, irritation tracing through her words. "It was his decision to drink. Whatever dilemma he was sorting through, he didn't want your help. He wanted no one's help."

A silence filled the room as everyone stared at their plates.

"I still never figured out why he was out so late at night," Channing said.

"Like James said, he had something on his mind. Something he wasn't willing to share with his family," Julianne said.

"Didn't the police find an overnight bag?" Channing asked.

"That's all been explained," Julianne said. "He sometimes stayed on board so as not to disturb me if he got in late. Now, eat up everybody. The crab's getting cold."

"Perhaps he was entertaining on board." James shot Channing a sly smile.

Julianne carefully placed her knife and fork down and folded her hands into her lap. "What are you implying?"

James shrugged. "I'm implying nothing. Simply that I know you were arguing and he needed a break."

"A break that involved somebody else?"

I cringed at the sharpness in Julianne's tone, and felt Helen kick me again.

"Why not?"

"Because he was my husband and he was loyal."

"Nag a man for too long and he'll go elsewhere for comfort," James said.

"I never nagged Blake."

"That's not what I heard," James muttered as he finished his wine and gestured at Channing to top up his glass.

"Then you heard wrong," Julianne said.

The tension in the room rose, along with my shoulders, as everybody focused on their food.

I looked over to see if Flipper was sensing anything strange. Now I knew Blake had died in interesting circumstances, his ghost could be lurking around the house.

Flipper was still focused on the food and didn't seem concerned about the possibility the ghost of Blake Carlisle was close by.

And I wasn't getting any ghostly vibes in the room, although the unpleasantly tense atmosphere could be wiping those out. Julianne kept shooting evil glares at James, who blatantly ignored her as he tucked into his food. Marcus was chewing furiously on an asparagus tip and Channing was reading the label on the back of the wine bottle.

Julianne pushed her food around her plate a few times before dropping her fork. "After dinner, I'll show you the views out the back of the house." She looked over at me. "We can take our dessert there."

"I'll look forward to that," I said.

"And I'll bring the accounts with me," Julianne said. "Run you through things. I'm not expecting you to do the books, but I want you to keep an eye on what's flowing out of the business. Make sure I'm not writing checks for unnecessary expenses."

"I can do all of that," Marcus said swiftly. "I'm good with money."

"You have other responsibilities," Julianne said. "There are three new accounts we need to close this week. You have to focus on that."

"I can do both."

"You don't need to now Lorna's here," Julianne said. She smiled at me. "Hope you have a good head for numbers."

"Of course. I'm happy to look at the books," I said. "I'll make sure you spend nothing you shouldn't." I repressed a smile as there was more grumbling from Marcus. He clearly didn't approve of being bossed around by two women. Well, tough. I was here and would do this job to the best of my abilities.

"And Helen, I've been on a splurge recently," Julianne said. "I need a few dresses tailored and have old ones that need taking in. I've lost weight in the last few months. Everything I wear hangs off me now."

Helen smiled brightly, never happier than when she was darning or tailoring outfits. "Not a problem. Just let me know what you need."

Julianne let out a sigh. "It's good to have more females in the house. It was getting a bit much having all the men here. All that testosterone flying around makes things tense and claustrophobic."

"You've got Honey," Channing said.

"Not for much longer," Julianne said. "Her contract ends in two months. I've already suggested she look for alternative employment. She worked with Blake, not me."

"You should give her a chance," Channing said. "She's a nice girl when you get to know her."

"I don't want to get to know her," Julianne said. "I never thought she was a good fit here. Blake only took her on because he felt sorry for her."

"And he completely ignored the fact she's stunning," James muttered.

"And half his age," Julianne said. "My husband was a decent man. He wouldn't be interested in somebody so young. It's not appropriate."

I looked around and saw several pairs of raised eyebrows at this comment. Perhaps Blake was interested in Honey as more than an assistant. And if Julianne had found out, it would be an excellent motive for her wanting rid of her husband. There was nothing worse than a woman betrayed.

There could be more to Blake's death than a drunken fall over the side of his yacht. Helen seemed to think so as well. She kept kicking me under the table and giving me wide-eyed looks.

Although Blake's ghost wasn't around, I wanted to learn more about this family, figure out what happened to Blake, and make sure it was nothing bad.

Falling overboard and drowning was horrible enough, but if someone had harmed him, I wanted to find out who and make sure they didn't get away with it.

Chapter 6

Honey arrived a few moments later to clear the plates. Flipper followed her to the door, hoping to get any leftovers. He looked disappointed when she didn't even glance at him before leaving with the dinner remains.

"Let's leave the men to it," Julianne said, nodding at Helen and me.

"That's no fun," Channing said, his bottom lip jutting out. "I much prefer female company."

"Because you're a girl," James said.

"No. Because they're much more interesting than you. Although that's never a challenge."

"No matter," Julianne said as she stood. "Tell Honey to bring our chocolate tortes to the back parlor. We can watch the sun set as we chat about business."

I walked alongside Julianne with Helen and Flipper. We all listened, as Julianne pointed out various family portraits.

"That stern-faced man was my great grandfather." She slowed by a painting of a man with a hooked nose and a scowl on his face. "He started the family interest in wine making."

"The vineyard sounds fascinating," Helen said. "What's the name of the business?"

"Firefly Vineyard." A soft smile crossed Julianne's face. "I love going on site. I can lose myself there for hours, strolling through the vines and checking on how everything is going. It took us a while to get the hang of things. Neither Blake nor I had experience in vineyards or wine production, but we both wanted to give it a go."

"I wouldn't know where to start," Helen said.

"It's not that tricky." Julianne showed us into a cream parlor with comfortable looking sofas scattered with cushions and throws. An open fireplace dominated one wall. "You work out how many vines you need, lay out your planting, dig enough holes, set up the trellis, and keep the pests at bay. The business was established when we took over, so it was a case of keeping on top of things and making sure the wine tastes good and people keep buying."

We settled on the sofas. Honey walked in a moment later with a tray of chocolate torte, plates, and dessert forks.

"We'll have coffee, as well." Julianne dismissed Honey with a wave of her hand as she set to serving the torte.

Honey turned without saying a word and stomped out of the room. I'd be cautious about drinking anything Honey served. She could lace it with something unpleasant to get revenge for being treated so coldly by Julianne.

"Isn't the view lovely?" Julianne scooped up a piece of torte as she gestured to the large bay window.

I turned my attention to the window and my breath caught in my throat. The sun was dipping into the sea, casting an amber glow across the water. I could see a dozen white boats as they bobbed on the waves. It looked like heaven.

"It's beautiful," Helen said around a large mouthful of torte. "And this is delicious."

"I get them from a bakery in the village," Julianne said. "They bake fresh there every day. It's always a popular place. You have to get your orders in early if you want anything."

"We must go there," Helen said, always the first to hunt out good places to find treats.

"How long have you lived here?" I asked Julianne.

"We moved here five years ago, after my father died unexpectedly. He was running the business until then. He'd taken over from my grandfather. I know the area well, having spent a lot of time here helping out over the summers when I was younger, before moving to London with Blake. I always had a hankering for coming back. When the vineyard needed a new owner, it was the perfect opportunity to return and try our hand at running a business."

"I can see why you'd want to return with a view like this," I said. "You don't miss London life?"

"I still have to go back to London regularly," Julianne said. "We supply some of the hotels with wine. But no, I can't say I miss it all that much. You can keep your crowded trains and high-powered jobs. Nothing beats this."

I finished my torte and put down my plate. "It must feel a little strange living here without your husband."

Julianne kept her gaze on the window. "It is. We'd been together a long time. His death was a big shock. I still expect him to walk through the front door, laughing and saying it was all some big mistake. Of course, that won't happen."

"What role did your husband have in the business?" I asked.

"A bit of everything really, although he focused on the financial side of things. He was amazing with people, though. He could make the most sullen person smile. And he had a great way of making new contacts and building connections. Our income has more than trebled over the last five years. That was all thanks to Blake and his ability to get people to warm to him."

"I'm sure you're doing a great job on your own," Helen said.

"And you have us here now," I said.

Julianne gave me a small smile. "Yes. And I'm not really alone. Blake's family is still around, as you can see by Channing's regular appearances. And Blake's old school friend, James, is often about. He helps with the business. Not with the day-to-day running, but he's got a good eye for an investment."

"And you have Marcus," Helen said, sneaking me a wry smile.

"Yes. He's always around, isn't he," Julianne said. "I'm yet to decide if that's a good thing. It might be time for a change of staff. He is good at what he does, but he's trying too hard. Blake spent years learning how to run a successful business. Marcus needs to slow down and learn how everything works before he steps into a more senior position. No matter how many times I tell him that it, doesn't stop him from asking me for a promotion at least once a month."

"Ambition isn't a bad thing," I said.

"You're right. I shouldn't complain. He is efficient. Although he can go too far at times. I think he'd pick out my clothes if I let him." Julianne shook her head. "Speaking of business and being efficient, perhaps you can take a quick look at the books now."

Stuffed full of excellent food, wine, and torte, all I wanted to do was kick back and enjoy the amazing view, but I needed to show I was keen and capable. "Of course. Let's take a look."

Julianne stood. "I won't be a minute. My study is at the end of the corridor."

The second she'd left, I sat forward and tapped Helen on the knee. "So, Blake's dead and there's a question over what happened to him."

Helen licked chocolate sauce from her fingers. "It's probably rude to ask for another slice of torte, isn't it?"

"Yes, it is. Focus on the family, not the food."

"But the food is so tasty."

I shook my head. "What did you make of all the talk about Blake?"

Helen tilted her head to one side. "The police ruled it an accident. Rumor suggests otherwise."

"It could have been a jealous employee who killed him."

"Or a jealous wife."

"Or a mistress!"

The door opened. Honey walked through with another tray in her hands, this time with cups and a cafetiere on top.

I gave her my warmest smile. "You can put the coffee on the table. And thanks for bringing it in. It's good of you."

Honey shrugged as she stepped back toward the door. "It's what Julianne expects of me."

"Maybe not what you expect to do, though?"

That earned me another shrug. "I need to keep my job here. Now Blake's not around, I have to turn my hand to anything that's asked of me."

"What work did you do for Blake?"

"I was his apprentice." Honey glanced nervously at the open door. "I want to start my own millinery business someday. He was helping me learn what it would take to do that."

"But you've gone from apprentice to kitchen server," I said. "That's not going to help you much in getting your hat making business off the ground. You can't be happy about that."

"I get paid. And you need money to start a business." Honey twisted her hands in front of her, her gaze on the floor.

"Perhaps you could speak to Julianne, let her know this isn't what you want to do."

"Everyone has to start somewhere," Honey said. "I should be grateful she's kept me on. You might have noticed, but we don't have the best of relationships."

"Maybe she's still sad about Blake's death," I said. "Grief makes people behave in strange ways. Had you known Blake for a long time?"

"For a while." Honey's gaze shot around the room as if seeking an escape route.

I opened my mouth to ask her another question, but heard footsteps hurrying back toward the room.

Honey gave us a quick nod, grabbed our empty plates, and ducked out the door.

"Here we are." Julianne strode into the room with her laptop under one arm and a file in her hand. "Let's get down to business."

My attention was still on Honey's speedy exit as Julianne gave me the file and opened her laptop. There was more to Honey's relationship with Blake than just being his apprentice. And why did Julianne hate her so much?

Somehow, Blake's death was tied up in these complicated relationships. But until he decided to show up in ghost form and help me figure out what was going on, I'd be left to puzzle it out with Helen and Flipper. And, right now, they were much more interested in the chocolate torte than working out what had happened to Blake.

Chapter 7

I woke early the next morning, grateful not to have had any more horrible dreams about being on board a sinking boat.

I was keen to use my free morning to go back to the Orwell and see if I could find any sign of Blake's ghost on board. Given the comments flying around the dinner table last night, there was unfinished business that he might need help with.

Tapping quietly on Helen's door, Flipper by my side, I jumped as she opened it straightaway, already dressed. "Great minds think alike. Are you planning a trip back to the marina?"

I nodded. "I think Blake might be waiting for us there. And I bet he'll have a few questions about how he died."

"Well, we've already got a few suspects if it turns out his death wasn't an accident." Helen shut her bedroom door and we hurried along the corridor, down the stairs, and over to her car. "Who's your favorite suspect so far?"

"I'm thinking Marcus." I opened the back door and let Flipper inside. "He's got an ambitious streak, and he's very controlling. Maybe he got frustrated that he couldn't control Blake."

"Have you sensed Blake's ghost in the house?"

"No. But from the way Flipper behaved yesterday when we were on the yacht, I think I missed something."

We zoomed out of the driveway and back along the narrow country lanes, which were thankfully quiet, given the early hour.

Parking in the marina car park, we hurried along the jetty to the Orwell and climbed on board the lower deck.

"Where do you want to start?" Helen asked.

"You stay up here so you don't get sick," I said. "Have a walk around and see if you sense anything strange, cold spots, that sort of thing. I'll take Flipper below and see if he can pick up on anything."

"Good plan." Helen took in a deep breath of air. "I'll stay right here. I won't think about the way the boat is moving and how my stomach's flipping over, making me glad we didn't have breakfast."

I grinned. "We'll be as quick as we can." I walked down the stairs and stopped in the lounge. Everything was neat and tidy, with a luxurious sofa covered in white scatter cushions and the table set with cutlery and plates. It looked more like a show boat than something that was used regularly.

"Do you sense anything strange?" I whispered to Flipper.

He looked up at me before sniffing around the room. So far, he seemed content.

I did a circuit, checking any areas for cold spots or places where I got lightheaded. There was nothing. Maybe Blake's death had been an accident and he hadn't stayed behind. There would be no reason to if he'd simply fallen overboard after having one too many drinks.

"Have you found anything down there?" Helen called out.

"Nothing so far." I looked over at Flipper, who was nosing behind a cushion. "How about you?"

He looked up at me, a potato chip sticking out of his mouth. Trust Flipper to find food rather than a ghost.

"I don't think there's anything down here," I muttered to myself. The Orwell felt normal. There was nothing odd or spooky about it.

I made my way back up the stairs with Flipper to find Helen hanging over the edge of the yacht, a green tinge to her skin. "Still not found your sea legs?"

"I don't know what's wrong with me," Helen said. "I'm not usually this bad. I blame last night's dinner. All that rich food is upsetting my stomach."

I looked around the deck. "It could be that you're the one sensing the ghost for a change."

"And he's making me sick?" Helen groaned. "If that's the case, you can stick your ghost detecting abilities. I want nothing to do with them."

"It happens to me sometimes," I said. "Normally, I get lightheaded or cold, but there have been a few ghosts who have made my stomach turn. They're usually the mean ones."

"We don't want any mean ghosts making contact."

"Ideally, we don't want any ghosts at all," I said.

"If this is Blake, tell him to stop," Helen said. "I feel like an idiot, getting sick every time I step on board. It's not at all ladylike."

"And green really isn't your color."

"Hilarious."

I ambled around the deck, trying to pick up any sense of a ghost.

Flipper whined and sat down, his gaze focused on the horizon.

I looked at him carefully and saw he was licking his lips. "Helen. I think Flipper's unwell too."

"He can join me here if he likes," Helen said. "The breeze is helping. If I keep my eyes on the horizon and don't move, this is perfect."

Flipper whined again, turning his sorrowful gaze to me before throwing up.

I grimaced as I sidestepped the vomit and petted his head. "You poor thing. It's okay. We'll be off here soon."

I was looking around for something to clean up the mess when my phone rang. I pulled it out and saw Zach's number.

For a second, I was tempted to ignore the call. We'd parted without making up after our silly fight about lost shoes and underwear, but we needed to smooth things over. This was an adult relationship and adults said sorry and moved past stolen underwear.

I answered the call.

"Good morning. I thought I'd check in and see how Cornwall's treating you." Zach's tone was as cautious as I felt.

"It's beautiful as always," I said, kneeling and stroking Flipper to reassure him everything was okay, and I wasn't angry at him for getting sick. "I'm just exploring the family's yacht."

"Sounds like fun," Zach said, his tone warming.

"I'm enjoying it, but Flipper keeps being sick on board."

"Is that him I can hear whining in the background?"

"It is." I ran my fingers through Flipper's fur. "I've never seen him like this before."

"You don't think he's ill?"

"Flipper will live forever." I knew that wasn't true, but the thought of Flipper getting ill and leaving me was one I was never prepared to consider.

"You haven't started work yet?"

"Not until this afternoon," I said. "Julianne will be away a lot, so I can work flexible hours."

"That's even better," Zach said. "When I come for a visit, you can show me around."

"I'd be happy to." I twisted my fingers together. "Listen, I didn't mean to accuse you of stealing my underwear. I just put it somewhere silly and forgot about it."

He let out a sigh. "Same goes for my stuff. And it's weird, but the same thing happened this morning. I absolutely put my watch on the bedside cabinet, but when I came out of the bathroom, it had gone."

"It's not Gunner having a joke with you?"

"He wouldn't do that," Zach said. "Besides, he was on a late shift last night and is still in bed."

"Maybe we have a poltergeist?"

"Don't even joke about that," Zach said. "One reason I built this house was so we wouldn't have any lingering ghostly residents who should have moved on."

"I sense nothing strange in our house," I said. "Well, there is a cold spot in the kitchen."

"You've said nothing about that before." Zach sounded worried.

"Because you'd worry if I did. And like you said, the house is new. We don't have any ghosts living with us."

He was silent for a second. "Unless the ghost is attached to you."

A shudder ran through me. "You think I've brought a ghost into the house?"

"I know nothing about it," Zach said. "Is that possible?"

"I'm no expert," I said. "I have no clue how the ghosts get here or where they go. I'm as much as an amateur as you."

"You're amazing at what you do," he said. "But I wondered, if the ghost isn't connected to the house, could it be someone you have a connection with? Or maybe any of us? Perhaps it's a ghost who has a link to me or Gunner. Could that happen?"

"Hold on. We don't even know there is a ghost," I said. "It could just be me forgetting where I put things."

"Maybe I could get the place exorcized while you're away. Just to be on the safe side."

"It's not a demon!" I said. At least, I hoped it wasn't, or we would put the house on the market in double quick time. "If it is a ghost, we can deal with it when I get back. You'll just have to put up with your watch going missing for a bit longer."

"I can live with that. You haven't met any ghosts down in Cornwall?"

"Not yet." I cast my gaze around the yacht. "But it is odd. Flipper is getting ill all the time and Helen's not doing so well when she sets foot on this yacht. It's like they're picking up on something."

"You've given Helen your ability to see ghosts?"

"It's not like that. You can't catch what I've got." I stood and walked to the side of the yacht, taking in the glorious views as the sun slid higher into the light clouds in the brilliant blue sky.

"So, what's different about this ghost if you're not picking it up but the others are?"

"I'm not even sure there is a ghost here," I said. "I'm not sure anyone came to harm. Julianne's husband, Blake, fell overboard, but the family reckon it was an accident."

I looked back at Flipper to see him washing his paws. He seemed more settled, so maybe his illness had nothing to do with a ghost.

I turned back and looked out at the open water. It was so beautiful here. It would be lovely not to have to worry about solving someone's murder.

"I'd better investigate this cold spot in the kitchen," Zach said. "If it's not a ghost, then it must be my shoddy building work that's the problem."

"I'm sure it's neither," I said. "And make sure you keep an eye on where you put your watch next time."

"Same goes for you and your underwear."

We said our goodbyes and I let out a relieved sigh. Everything was fine between us. I pocketed my phone and looked at Helen. "Are you ready to go? I don't think we'll find anything helpful here."

"I was ready ten minutes ago. I'm not getting the hang of life aboard this yacht. I need firm ground beneath my feet."

"So, the chance of you hooking up with one of the millionaires in the yacht club and going sailing around the world is off the table?"

"I don't think Gunner would like me to do that."

"I didn't know you needed to ask his permission to date." I walked over to Helen.

Flipper brushed against my legs and I reached down to pet his head, but he wasn't there.

I turned and looked around, surprised to see he was still sitting in the same place, washing his paws. A shiver ran through me.

Helen touched my arm. "The color has drained from your face. Have you sensed something?"

"Standing in this spot, I do feel something odd."

"I'm glad it's not just me," Helen said.

"It feels different from your normal ghost." I looked around the deck. "And I could have sworn Flipper just walked past me and his fur brushed my leg."

"Could it be a child ghost?" she asked. "They brushed their fingers on you when they passed."

"No, it's not a child. It doesn't feel like a ghost at all." The yacht shifted beneath us and I grabbed hold of the rail.

"Let's get off here," Helen said. "Whatever it is, none of us like it. I'm just grateful I didn't eat anything before we came out."

"Me too." Even my stomach was unsettled. I gave the sea one final appreciative glance. As I did so, I felt an icy cold shove on my back.

I lost my grip on the railing and pitched over the side of the yacht.

Chapter 8

It was like my nightmare had just come true in horrifying technicolor. The water was icy cold as I plunged in, and I repressed the urge to scream as my head went under.

I broke the surface and gasped, flailing around and trying to grab hold of something to keep me from going under again. The drop from the top deck must have been twenty feet, and my skin tingled from the impact of hitting the water.

Helen's anxious looking face appeared over the side of the yacht. "You okay?"

"No! I just got shoved overboard." I took a few calming deep breaths. Despite the shock, I wasn't hurt, just a little winded. But the sea had barely a ripple on it, and I was a decent swimmer. I wasn't in any danger.

"Is there anything I can do to help?" Helen yelled.

I saw Flipper next to her, getting ready to jump in and be a hero dog. "Grab hold of Flipper and make sure he doesn't come in. I can get myself out."

"I'll find an inflatable to throw you." Helen hauled Flipper away from the edge of the yacht. A few seconds later, a red float appeared, and I grabbed hold of it.

Now I had the float, I was less panicked and just felt stupidly embarrassed. I spotted a ladder next to the mooring and waved at Helen before pointing to the ladder and kicking through the water.

I'd almost reached the ladder, when something huge and gray flew through the air off the side of the jetty, and landed next to me.

I screamed and spluttered, almost losing my grip on the float, before coming face to face with an enormous husky.

The dog grabbed hold of my collar and dragged me toward the jetty.

A few seconds later, the curly haired woman I'd seen at the Carlisles' house appeared. "Hey! Are you hurt? I saw you fall in and thought you might need help."

"I'm okay." I petted the husky, hoping he'd let me go.

"Brutus is trained in search and rescue. He almost yanked my arm off when he saw you go overboard. It's in his blood to help people."

We reached the ladder. Brutus remained in the water as I slowly climbed up. "Well, thanks for rescuing me. It was a shock pitching over like that."

Brutus leaped onto the jetty and showered us both with seawater as he shook his fur.

Helen hurried over with Flipper by her side and a large fluffy pink towel over her arm.

"Did someone push you in?" The woman cast a suspicious glance at Helen.

"No! I must have tripped." I shot Helen a warning look willing her not to say anything about ghosts as I took the towel.

"Really?" The woman looked up at the side of the yacht. "That must have been quite some trip to go straight over the railings like that."

"I am accident prone." I rubbed my hair with the towel. "I'm Lorna Shadow, by the way. I've just started working for Julianne Carlisle."

"Nice to meet you. I'm Taylor."

"I saw you yesterday," I said. "Were you at the Carlisle house?"

Taylor smiled. "That's right. Mrs. Carlisle is interested in getting a new dog. I'm known around the village because I train dogs and own a few of my own. Brutus is one of six dogs in my pack."

"That's a lot of dogs," Helen said.

"I find them more faithful than men," Taylor said. "And they're so easy to train. Again, more so than men." She petted Brutus on the head.

I grinned at her. "I can't argue with that."

"And who's this?" Taylor looked at Flipper.

"He's mine," I said and made the introductions. "Oh, and this is Helen."

Helen scowled at me, but she was used to me putting Flipper before her. Taylor smiled at Helen as she petted Flipper. "He's a handsome boy."

"And he knows it," I said.

Taylor stepped back. "They always do. I think I have my dogs well-trained, but they've got me wrapped around their beautiful paws. I've devoted my life to them. But they make me happy, so why not?"

I instantly liked Taylor. Anyone obsessed with animals was all right in my books.

"Well, I must go. I've got dog walks to do. And I'm spending the afternoon with a six-month-old puppy, teaching him the delights of how to sit and stay."

"Thanks again for saving me." I waved Taylor and Brutus goodbye.

"Are you sure you're okay?" Helen asked, once Taylor was out of earshot. "You didn't trip, did you?"

"I didn't. And it wasn't someone living who shoved me in either." I wrung water out of my hair. "It felt like I got shoved in the back by someone small."

"I told you it was the ghost of a child on the yacht," Helen said.

"No one's mentioned a child dying. I was expecting to find Blake's ghost here. A ghost child will complicate things."

The sound of running footsteps made me look up. It was Marcus and Honey barrelling toward us.

"Is everything okay?" Marcus stopped by my side.

"Everything's fine." I rubbed my hands over my sodden clothes. "I just had an accident."

"That was quite a fall." Honey turned her wide eyes to the yacht. "And that was the exact same place where Blake fell overboard."

"It was?" I looked back at the yacht. "Blake fell from that exact spot?"

"Well, close enough," Marcus said. "No one saw him fall, but that's where the police think he fell over. They found smeared prints as if he'd tried to cling to the railing but couldn't get back on board."

"It was easy to get out from where I fell in," I said. "Even without the help of the float and that dog, I could have swum to the ladder. It's no distance."

"Maybe not so easy in the middle of the night if you'd been drinking," Marcus said, his hands hovering over me and his forehead wrinkled. "We need to get you some dry clothes. You look a fright."

"I'm okay," I said. "But I'd better get back to the house and get changed."

"I insist," Marcus said. "We keep clothes on the yacht. I'll have you dry in an instant."

Reluctantly, I followed Marcus back on board and he disappeared below deck. I wasn't so sure about being on the deck after what had just happened.

I looked around carefully, but couldn't see any sign of my ghostly attacker.

"Get changed below deck." Marcus reappeared and handed me two more clean towels. "I've laid out clothes for you."

Despite his officiousness, I appreciated Marcus's help. I headed below deck, washed the salt out of my hair and changed into the clothes. Marcus had selected a cream sleeveless dress and pale pink short-sleeved cardigan for me. It was more the sort of thing Helen would wear, but all I cared about was that it was dry.

When I returned to the lounge, Marcus had made tea for everyone, and I could smell toast. My stomach grumbled.

He smiled at me and ran an appreciative gaze over my outfit. "It looks like it was made for you. Join us. None of us have had any breakfast. There's plenty of food on board."

I accepted a cup of tea from him as I sat at the table where Honey and Helen were sitting, happily munching on toast.

"What made you both come to the yacht so early?" Marcus asked.

Flipper followed him around as he made more toast, no doubt hoping to get some of his own, all thoughts of his upset stomach seeming to have gone. Nothing stopped Flipper when there was the opportunity to grab food.

"Oh, nothing in particular. We just wanted another look around," I said.

"I'm the same," Marcus said. "I love it here. I brought Honey along because there's a cleaning job going at the club I thought she might be good at."

Honey snitched her nose. "I'm not ready to leave the house just yet."

I smiled at Honey. "You didn't get the chance to tell me what you and Blake were working on last night."

Honey placed her cup down. "After I left college, I struggled to get a job. Blake was kind enough to offer me work experience. He paid me and gave me a room in the house. He was showing me how the business operated. I was learning a lot."

"Has that changed now you're working for Julianne?" Helen asked.

"It has. She hates me," Honey said. "She'll be glad when I'm gone. And I'll go as soon as I can, but I have nowhere to live. I'm looking around, but everything is so expensive here. I might move farther away. But I've grown to love the place. I'll be sad to leave."

"I'm sure Julianne doesn't hate you," I said. "She'll give you time before you have to move out."

"You saw how she treated me yesterday," Honey said. "And now Blake's gone, she's got me doing domestic work rather than learning about the business. I'll get out as soon as I can afford to."

Marcus hurried over from the kitchen with a plate of toast and a fresh pot of tea. "Julianne has old-fashioned values when it comes to running the business. She prefers men to be in charge."

"Which is why she wants me to look at the accounts." I shook my head as I helped myself to toast.

"Well, that is all rather odd," Marcus said, his eyebrows shooting up. "I'm sure she's still grieving after losing Blake. She's made some strange decisions recently."

"You consider me to be a strange decision?" I asked.

"Oh, no! I didn't mean that. I'm sure you're excellent at what you do." Marcus dashed away before bringing back a tray of preserves. "It's just that, well, Blake was grooming me to take over the business."

"Is that so?"

"Absolutely." Marcus sat next to Honey. "They don't have children and he was looking for someone to carry on his excellent work. He knew I could be relied upon."

"He couldn't have been thinking of retiring," Helen said. "How old was he?"

"Only a few years older than Julianne," Honey said. "Blake was in his early forties. And he wasn't talking about retiring. He loved Firefly Vineyard. I always imagined he'd be working there until he was old and gray." She sniffed and her gaze dropped.

"If he was going to carry on running the business for decades," I said to Marcus, "you were prepared to wait that long before taking over?"

Marcus focused on his toast. "I got the impression he was winding down, spending more time with the family. He needed someone to oversee day-to-day things. That was how I was planning on starting out."

"Before you took over completely?" I arched an eyebrow.

"It takes years to learn how to run a business like this," Marcus said. "And I'm in no hurry. Blake paid me well and I enjoyed his company. I was happy to help out however I could."

"But now he's gone." Honey placed her knife down. "So, neither of us will ever find out what he really wanted."

"I'm certain he'd want me to remain here," Marcus said, giving a quick nod. "There's only so much I can learn from Julianne. I'm planning on making a formal recommendation to the board that I take on the director role of the company by the end of the year."

Honey looked at him in alarm. "Julianne doesn't want to give up the business. She loves it as much as Blake did."

"Why do you care what Julianne wants?" Marcus asked. "She's horrible to you."

"Even so, you can't kick her out of the company. She's under enough stress having just lost Blake."

"I'm not kicking anyone out," Marcus said. "You don't understand how this works."

"Then explain it to us." Despite Marcus's excellent tea and toast making skills, he was annoying me.

"It's important the vineyard is well run." Marcus shuffled the preserves around on the table, lining them up in a neat row. "I was thinking Julianne could take on a figurehead role. Be the name of the company, shake the right hands, that sort of thing. She should hand over the running to me and make sure it's done properly."

"Julianne already runs things well," Honey said.

"But my ideas will modernize things. We could double turnover."

"Blake didn't like your ideas," Honey said.

"You know nothing about the business." Marcus patted Honey's hand. "You stick to what you're good at."

"Which is what?"

"Looking beautiful and being charming." Marcus smiled at us all, expecting his compliments to be well-received.

Honey stood from her seat. "If you'll excuse me, I need some air." She stomped away and up the stairs.

Marcus watched her go, a smile on his face, before turning to us. "She isn't all that bright, but I enjoy Honey's company when she isn't trying to do anything that impacts the business."

I bit the inside of my mouth. "She seems very nice."

"Blake thought so as well." Marcus leaned closer. "Did you know, she was more than just his assistant?"

"He was having an affair with Honey?" It was a thought I'd had myself.

"Isn't she too young for him?" Helen asked.

"Blake was a powerful man. Young women like that. That's why I model myself on Blake." Marcus straightened the cuffs on his shirt. "I want to be just like him."

If Honey and Blake had been having an affair, that also made her a suspect. "You know for sure they were together?"

Marcus shrugged. "It was obvious they were fond of each other. And he bought her presents."

"That doesn't mean they were sleeping together," Helen said. "I've had gifts from men in the past and didn't so much as give them a kiss on the cheek."

"Julianne was sure of the affair, as well," Marcus said.

"That's why she hates Honey so much," I said. "She thinks Honey was trying to take Blake away from her."

"It used to drive Julianne mad when she saw them together," Marcus said. "Blake would take Honey on business trips. Julianne knew they were more than business acquaintances."

"Did she ever confront Blake about it?" I asked.

"Not that I know of," Marcus said. "But Julianne wanted a divorce. She was so convinced he was cheating on her that she'd decided to leave him."

"How do you know that?"

"Oh, well, I found divorce paperwork when I was looking through a file. By accident, of course." Marcus stuffed a piece of toast into his mouth and chewed vigorously.

More like he was snooping around, trying to find dirt on the family. My opinion of Marcus declined. "So, if Julianne was planning to divorce Blake, she can't be sad that he died. I imagine he left everything to her in his will?"

"She got the house and the business," Marcus said. "It's a shame. I hoped he'd leave me something. I've worked for this company for years."

"That is a tragedy." My acerbic tone was clear.

"But I'm still here, and I plan to be here for a long time. And I will get everything Blake had." Marcus looked around the yacht, a gleam in his eyes.

"Does that include Honey?" Helen asked.

"She's a beautiful young woman," Marcus said, a faint blush on his cheeks. "She would be foolish not to consider me."

"You want Honey?" I couldn't hide my surprise.

"Why not?" he said. "She has nowhere to go and no prospects. She should be grateful I'd even consider her as the future Mrs. Patel."

"I'm sure that's exactly what she thinks." I caught Helen's eye and smirked.

Marcus brushed crumbs from his fingertips. "I'll even give her a little job to keep her amused. Nothing too taxing. I'm not sure there's much going on in that pretty head of hers. But I want to make sure she's occupied. She seems to like to work."

"Go figure," I said.

"I'll make fresh tea, shall I?" Marcus gathered the plates. "Get some air with Honey. I'll bring the tea up on deck."

"Good idea." At least Marcus wasn't old-fashioned when it came to getting his hands dirty in the kitchen. Honey wasn't condemned to a life of kitchen maid if Marcus ever made good on his creepy promise to claim her as his.

I followed Helen up the stairs onto the top deck and spotted Honey at the back of the yacht, her hands gripping the railing and her hair blowing in the breeze.

"What do you think of Marcus's claim about an affair?" I said to Helen.

"We'd thought it ourselves. And it would make Honey a suspect in Blake's death," she said. "A jealous lover wants more than a few nights of passion. Maybe Blake got tired of her and told Honey it was over. She got angry and shoved him overboard."

"Or Julianne found out what they were doing," I said.

"And what about Marcus?" Helen cast a glance over her shoulder. "Do you think he's ambitious enough to get rid of his boss and try to fill his shoes? It sounds like he wants everything Blake had, the business, the girlfriend, the fancy house, and the yacht. What's to say he won't go after Julianne next?"

"I don't know if Marcus has it in him to kill now I've spent more time with him. Although Julianne's definitely got the measure of him," I said. "She doesn't trust Marcus. Perhaps she's picked up on his desire to take over."

"I still think he could have snuck up on this yacht and shoved Blake overboard," Helen said. "It's the sort of sly thing he would do. He didn't want to get his hands dirty but needed Blake gone."

"He is unpleasantly ambitious. We'll keep an eye on him." I looked around the deck. "Now, if we can just find Blake and see what he has to say about all of this, we can figure things out."

"There's still no ghost popping up to offer unhelpful gestures and mimes for you to puzzle through?"

"Not that I can see," I said. "How are you feeling? Picking up anything odd?"

"Like my toast wants to come back up but nothing ghostly."

"Let's get off here," I said. "We need to get back to the house, anyway. And I'm not feeling comfortable wearing Julianne's clothes. I want to get changed."

"Suits me," Helen said.

"We'll pass on the tea," I said to Marcus, as he climbed up the stairs with a full tray of cups and a teapot. "We must get back and start our first day of work."

"That's such a shame," Marcus said. "Are you sure I can't tempt you? I've made Darjeeling."

"Thanks. Some other time." I caught a flash of movement out of the corner of my eye, and turned.

It was a dog, but it wasn't Flipper. There was a large, black, friendly looking Labrador sitting on the deck.

It was a ghost dog.

I took a step toward the dog. It gave me a startled look before disappearing.

Flipper ran over to where the dog had been and sniffed around. He looked at me and whined.

"Is everything okay?" Marcus asked. "You appear a little paler than normal."

"I just saw..." I rubbed my eyes. There had definitely been a ghost dog on the deck. I couldn't have imagined that. "Never mind. Just a trick of the light."

Marcus stared at the empty deck. "Well, it was lovely spending time with you, ladies. I shall see you at the house later and make sure you're settled in with everything you need."

I gave him a brief wave goodbye and hurried off the yacht with Helen and Flipper before dashing to the car.

"What's up?" Helen unlocked the car. "Did you see something on the Orwell?"

I nodded, glancing back at the yacht. "I just saw my first ghost dog."

Chapter 9

I explained what I'd seen to Helen as we drove back to the house.

"Wow! A ghost dog. Imagine that. It's not such a stretch of the imagination, since people come back when they have unfinished business. Why should it be any different for animals?"

"Why is there a ghost dog hanging about on the yacht?" I asked. "And why push me into the sea?"

"Maybe you scared him. And dogs can be territorial. Perhaps he doesn't like strangers coming on board."

"But... I love dogs."

"The ghost dog doesn't know that," Helen said. "All he saw was two strangers and their dog wandering about on his patch."

"Maybe that's why Flipper is getting so ill. He might have seen this ghost straightaway and has been reacting to it badly." I glanced into the back seat, but Flipper was already fast asleep.

"That makes sense. But I doubt that explains my own terrible sea sickness."

"You just need better sea legs."

"My legs are fine as they are." Helen shot around a corner in the car. "Maybe the dog was a family pet. He could still be hanging around waiting for its master. The poor thing might not even know Blake is dead. That would be so sad. How are you going to tell him he's lost his owner?"

"We don't know for sure this dog has anything to do with the family."

Helen pulled into the driveway and we climbed out of the car.

"I'll see what I can find out from Julianne today," I said. "It sounds like she likes dogs, so it'll be an easy enough topic to discuss."

After a quick change of clothes, I hurried to Julianne's office with Flipper to start my first afternoon of work.

Her office was all white, from the carpet to the desk. There was the occasional splash of red dotted around and two pale pink orchids, but other than that, it felt like I was working in an angel's office. I half expected harp music to start playing.

I found a note on the desk from Julianne. She'd be back in three hours and suggested I look through everything and familiarize myself with the filing system and computer.

After an hour of checking through the computer, I'd recognized all the programs, and the filing looked straightforward enough.

I opened the accounting files and scanned through them. This would keep me busy for a while as I worked through the company's outgoings. I checked through two months of statements and saw nothing strange. Regular payments to suppliers, staff wages, nothing out of the ordinary.

The ghost dog kept playing on my mind. He'd been surprised to find me on the yacht. He must have a connection to the family, or maybe it was to the yacht. Perhaps Blake had accidentally bought the vessel complete with its own ghost!

I walked around the room, looking for any photographs or clues that the ghost dog once lived here. There was nothing other than a few family photographs. No sign of dog toys, or beds, or pictures of pets.

The office door opened. Julianne walked in. She smiled when she saw me. "How you getting on? Everything making sense?"

"Fine, thanks." I decided not to mention my accident on board the Orwell. "I've been having a look at how everything works and it all makes sense."

"It's not too complicated for you?" Julianne sat at the desk and unwrapped a pale pink silk scarf from around her neck.

"No. It looks easy enough." I sat in the seat she gestured to.

"I like to keep things organized," Julianne said. "Blake was the ideas man, but I looked at the fine details. And it's important to know where everything is, so you don't make a mistake."

"It sounds like you're on top of things."

"Most of the time. But it can get overwhelming. I'm planning to employ more staff soon at the processing site. That always comes with extra headaches."

"I can help with that if you'd like me to."

"That would be great," Julianne said. "From the looks of your resume, you can turn your hand to everything."

"Just never leave me alone with a drill or a hammer," I said. "And I leave all the cooking to Helen. But give me an admin task, and I'm all yours."

"I'm much the same. I left all the DIY to Blake to organize and oversee." Her smile faded. "I'll need to do it all now."

"Not everything," I said. "I'm here to help. And, I promise, Helen will transform your closet and fix any stains or tears. She's a genius with that sort of thing. And anytime you need a homemade brownie, she's the woman to go to."

Julianne sat up straight in her seat. "You're right. Absolutely. I'm being foolish. It's only been two months since Blake died. I'm still getting used to things being so different."

"You must miss him."

She blinked at me. "I do. But our relationship was... complicated."

There seemed to be a lot of that going around. "Marriages often are."

"You're right there." Her smile was rueful. "Are you married?"

"Not yet." My thoughts flashed to the ring I'd discovered in Zach's sock drawer. "But I'm with someone. He's a lovely guy. Before that, it was just me and Flipper for a long time."

"I'm thinking about getting another dog. A companion would be nice," Julianne said. "Someone loyal, who you know will be on your side no matter what happens."

"That's why I love Flipper so much," I said, glancing over to where he slept. "You don't have any pets?"

"Not anymore," Julianne said. "Our last dog died recently. That was why I had Taylor visit yesterday to help me decide what breed of dog to get next. She suggested a Tibetan Terrier or a Cockapoo. Something that doesn't shed."

Flipper stood and paced to the window, his ears pricked and his tail up.

I followed his movement, my eyes widening as I spotted the ghost dog appear and sit next to him.

I was about to ask Julianne more about her old dog, when her phone rang. She checked the number before disconnecting the call. "I'd like you to start by getting my correspondence up-to-date. There are still a few people who don't know about Blake. I'm getting mail from them. I'd like that to stop. Make sure they know to contact me for all matters relating to the vineyard. If it's just sales stuff, get our details taken off their mailing list."

"I can deal with that." I dragged my attention away from the ghost dog.

"There's a few days' work involved with that. Then I want you to focus on the accounts. Make sure Blake was on top of things before he died. I'm sure we can reduce our outgoings. I'd like to do that so we can employ new staff as soon as possible."

Her phone rang again. She stared at the number before disconnecting it once more.

Someone wanted to speak to Julianne, and she wasn't keen. "I don't mind if you need to take that."

"It's nothing that can't wait." Julianne sighed and sat back in her seat. The desk phone rang and she snatched it up. "Firefly Vineyard."

I watched as her eyes narrowed and her hand clenched into a fist. Whoever she was speaking to wasn't a friend.

"Now's not a good time," Julianne said. "You may contact my assistant to arrange an appointment for when we may speak."

I looked over to the window. The ghost dog still sat with Flipper. From the unhappy look on Flipper's face, he wasn't feeling good. I needed to figure out how to get rid of this ghost dog fast to make sure Flipper didn't keep getting sick.

I jumped as Julianne slammed down the phone. "Some people have no manners." She shoved her chair back and stood. "I need a break."

I raised my eyebrows. She'd only been here ten minutes. "Is there anything you want me to do while you're gone?"

"Take a look through the yellow file on my desk." Julianne hurried to the door. "That's the correspondence you need to start with." She pulled open the door and left the room.

Whoever that caller was, they'd rattled Julianne. Someone after money? An unhappy customer? Or something more serious. Perhaps someone knew about Blake's affair with Honey and was trying to blackmail Julianne so the secret wouldn't come out.

I mulled over the options as I stood and walked over to Flipper and the ghost dog. "You've made a new friend."

Flipper looked at the ghost dog, laid his head back on his paws and heaved a sigh.

I stroked his head. "I'm not sure you want him around, though."

Flipper gave a gentle whine and his gaze shifted to the ghost dog.

The dog was looking at me with interest, so I held my hand out and felt my fingers chill as his nose touched my skin.

"Were you the one on the yacht? Did you push me overboard?"

The dog tried to lick my fingers, but all I got was an icy cold sensation running across my skin.

"You're welcome to hang around with us, but don't sit so close to Flipper. You're making him feel unwell."

The ghost dog nuzzled Flipper's paw before taking a step away. It looked like he understood me. Now, if I could figure out what he wanted and his connection to this family, he could go to his next life, or wherever ghost animals went.

Then, I could focus on what had happened to Blake.

Chapter 10

Julianne never returned that afternoon. I remained in the office for the rest of the day, sorting paperwork and writing drafts of letters.

Tidying the papers, I decided to call it a day. I left the office and walked up to my bedroom.

There was no sign of Helen, so I headed to her favorite place, the kitchen. She stood by the Aga, but she wasn't cooking. She was texting.

"Are you ordering takeout?" I sat at the island in the center of the kitchen.

Flipper curled up by the Aga, his ghostly friend staying by his side.

"Don't be silly. We never have takeout," Helen said, her gaze still on her phone. "I've got something cooking."

"Who are you messaging?"

"No one important." She stuffed her phone into her pocket. "How was your afternoon with Julianne?"

"Not great," I said. "I hardly saw her."

"No clues about our mystery dog?"

"I think he belongs to the family," I said. "Julianne mentioned a dog but then took a phone call and vanished. And she wasn't happy with whoever she spoke to."

Helen sat opposite me. "What did they want? Money, maybe?"

"That's what I wondered. If it's not money related, it could have something to do with Blake."

Helen sat forward in her seat. "Someone is after a story about him being unfaithful with Honey? Maybe they're going to sell it and make money off the family."

"That would hardly make front-page news," I said.

"It would around here. Villagers love to gossip."

"I wondered about that, but we're not talking a royal family marriage scandal. We're talking local businessman and his assistant. The most you'd sell that story for is a bag of chips and a free drink."

Helen wrinkled her nose. "I'd read the story."

I swatted her arm. "Let's hope it isn't that. I feel sorry for Julianne. She seemed overwhelmed when we were talking earlier. It must be hard losing someone so unexpectedly."

Helen's phone vibrated and she pulled it out and smiled. "Just give me a second. I need to reply to this."

"Exactly who are you texting?"

"Like I said, no one important." She grinned as she read the message and then shot back a quick reply.

"Does this unimportant person have a name?"

"I don't remember." Helen's phone vanished into her lap. "So, we have Julianne the grieving wife, Honey the mistress, and Marcus who wants to take over Blake's business. If he was murdered, they're all suspects."

"And the ghost dog," I said.

"We can't include a dog as a murder suspect," Helen said. "You can't try him in court."

"I was wondering if he pushed Blake over." I ran my hands through my hair. "This could all be a sad accident. The dog knocked Blake over by mistake, same thing he did to me this morning. Dogs can get over-excited and jump up at people. If Blake had been drunk and lost his hold on the railing, it could have happened that way."

"If that did happen, no wonder the dog doesn't want to leave, knowing he killed his owner. How are you going to figure that one out?"

"I've also had another idea. It's one I don't want to dwell on, but we need to consider it."

"What's that?"

"Blake jumped off. It all got too much for him and he decided life at the bottom of the ocean was better than whatever stress he was under."

"That's pretty dark." Helen wrapped her arms around herself. "Surely things can't have been that bad for him. He lived in an amazing house and ran a successful business. Why throw that away?"

"I'm not sure yet. And from a look at the accounts, the business is doing well. Maybe Blake wasn't happy about something. If his affair had been discovered and someone was blackmailing him, it could have gotten too much and that was the only way out he could see."

"Still no sign of Blake?" Helen asked. "You can run these ideas past him and see what he thinks."

"Nothing," I said. "The ghost dog is the only spook around."

Helen's phone vibrated again. She jumped up, a grin on her face, as she yanked her phone out and inspected the message.

I grabbed it before she could reply to the message. "Who's it from?"

"Give that back." Helen snatched at the phone, but I held on tight.

My eyes widened. "Why are you texting Gunner?"

"He asked me to." Helen's cheeks went bright pink.

I grinned at her. "Are you two having a secret relationship?"

"We're not. I would never keep something like that from you," Helen said, as I handed back her phone. "But we are talking."

"About what?"

"All sorts of things," she said. "We're getting to know each other."

"You *are* having a relationship with Gunner!"

"I'm taking my text messaging outside." Helen pouted at me before flouncing out the back door.

Grinning at her retreating form, I was glad they were sorting things out. It had been a long time coming. The first time Helen had seen Gunner, she'd blushed and fumbled her words, so I knew there was something about him she liked. But he was so different from the type she thought she found attractive. Helen always professed to being into posh guys with big bank accounts. Gunner was the opposite of that. But if he made her happy, that was all I cared about.

I stood and inspected the contents of the pot on the Aga. There were some chopped potatoes in there, but they were uncooked. I pulled open the door to the Aga and black smoke came out.

Coughing, I backed away, waving my hand in front of my face. It looked like Gunner's texts had been a bit too distracting for Helen. She never burned dinner.

I was looking around for something to use to get the burning pie out, when the kitchen door opened and James barged through.

"What's burning? Is there a fire?" His gaze shot around the kitchen.

"Don't worry." I used a cloth to yank the pie out. "It's just our dinner."

James squinted at me and then approached the Aga. "I never could figure out how to use these wretched things." He jabbed a finger at the smoking pie. "You'll be eating cold tonight. That thing isn't worth saving."

"Or takeout."

"We'll have none of that," James said, straightening his crumpled jacket. "Let me take you both out to dinner. We can celebrate your arrival and my recent win on the horses."

I raised my eyebrows, surprised by his generosity. "You don't need to do that."

"I'm happy to take two lovely ladies out to dinner," he said. "And I don't suppose you've seen much of the village yet."

"Not yet," I said.

"Then it's a date," James said. "I know a lovely fish restaurant overlooking the sea. And you can sample some of our wine while we're there. They're a stockist."

"Sounds good," I said. "We just need to wait for Helen to get back from texting her... man friend." I wasn't sure what to call Gunner, since they weren't technically official.

James pulled a mock frown. "Don't tell me you're both taken?"

I scratched my head. "We both are, sort of."

"Oh well, dinner as friends will have to do." He patted my arm. "Actually, I've got my eye on a girl in the village. I haven't convinced her to go on a date with me yet, but I'm wearing her down."

"Maybe romance is the way to go," I said. "I'm not sure being worn down would ever be an incentive for me to go on a date with somebody."

James laughed. "A good point. Flowers and chocolates it is."

"Is it okay if I bring Flipper?" He looked like he needed time out from his ghostly buddy. He still seemed under the weather. The ghost dog hadn't left his side since it had materialized.

"Not a problem," James said. "There's an outside eating area. And it's such a lovely evening. Find your friend and we can go fill our faces. Then I will tell you all the gossip about the family."

The evening sounded even more promising. We left the burnt pie on the counter. I grabbed Helen and we met James at the front of the house.

"Hop in, girls." James jumped into the driver's seat of a sporty black Jaguar. "Let me titillate your taste buds."

"I like the sound of that," Helen said as we climbed in.

James sped away from the house. "I couldn't leave you and Lorna to eat a charred pie. It might have made you unwell."

"I promise you, that was a one off. I never spoil food. But I got distracted by an urgent matter." She shot me an apologetic look.

"Well, I'm glad you did," James said. "I always like to get to know the new staff. The business is a friendly place to work. We have no airs and graces. People muck in when they need to. Although, I prefer to watch from the sidelines." He gave us a grin.

"Have you worked with Julianne for long?" I asked.

"Not really," James said. "I know her well, of course. But most of my dealings were with Blake. Now he's gone, I'm seeing if Julianne and I can work together. I come here once a week for a couple of days to run through business matters, check investments, that sort of thing. So far, it's going well."

"How are you connected to their business?"

"I'm a wine merchant," James said, "and a silent partner. I helped Blake when he was getting going, gave him the start-up capital. I never wanted to run my own business, but I'm happy to reap the rewards when someone is successful. Blake had a passion for wine, just like me. I especially like drinking the stuff."

"We've yet to see the vineyard," I said.

"It's a marvelous place," James said. "And it's the perfect time of year to see it. Grape harvesting is underway. Our first new batch should be bottled by the end of the week. But it's the vintage stuff you really want. There are a few bottles in the cellar worth sampling. I keep some in the hope I'll get a collector's item one day. You can make a fortune off a good vintage."

"I do enjoy a good bottle of wine," Helen said.

"Then that will be our next date," James said. "I'll take you to the vineyard and show you around."

We drove for the next ten minutes, chatting about the vineyard. James was a friendly guy. I hoped we'd get him on the subject of what had really happened to Blake on the Orwell.

"This is the place." James pulled up outside a whitewashed wooden building, the window frames painted pale blue and wooden seagulls dotted around everywhere. "I'll sort us a table on the balcony at the back. It's the best view around."

We followed him into the restaurant and waited as James chatted up the manager before beckoning us to follow him. He led us onto a decked area with half a dozen tables. Several people were already sitting out there, and we chose a quiet table in the corner.

I settled in my seat and took a moment to appreciate the view. It was incredible, with the azure blue sea sparkling and yachts bobbing on the waves.

"I recommend the sea bass," James said as he sat down. "It comes with a lemon sauce to die for."

"That sounds yummy," Helen said.

"Unless you're into oysters. They get them fresh every day."

I wrinkled my nose. Slimy, still living sea critters sliding down my throat was my idea of hell. "I'm not such an oyster fan."

"Neither am I." James studied the wine menu. "But people insist they're wonderful, so I oblige occasionally."

The young waitress arrived to take our order. We all chose the sea bass along with fresh local vegetables.

"We'll take two bottles of the Firefly Reserve. 2005 if you have that in the cellar."

The waitress nodded and hurried away.

"I'm not much of a drinker," I said. More than two glasses of anything alcoholic and I saw double.

"Good job I am," James said, with a grin. "One of you girls will need to drive the Jag home later. I intend to enjoy myself tonight."

"I've never driven a Jaguar," Helen said. "I'd love to get behind the wheel of yours."

"Then my keys are yours," James said. "So long as you get us back to the house safely, that's all I care about."

Helen grinned at me and rubbed her hands together.

I repressed a grimace. Helen in charge of something so powerful would be a frightening thing.

"I was sorry to hear about what happened to Blake," I said, deciding it was time to steer the conversation to a useful topic.

"Darned shame, that's what it was," James said.

We waited as the waitress returned and poured the wine. James sampled it and gave a hearty nod.

"Excellent, as always. And so it should be, since it's one of ours."

After the waitress left and we'd all tasted the wine, I tried again. "You mentioned at dinner that you were surprised by how Blake died."

"A terrible thing," James said. "To fall over the side of your own yacht. And then to not be able to get out of the water. It just doesn't seem believable."

"What else could have happened?" I asked.

"I wish I knew," he said. "We'd not been speaking much just before he died. We'd been friends all these years and then had a silly falling out over some business matter. The last thing I said to him was spoken in anger and I regret that. That's why I'm questioning his death. I still want him here, so we can make up and forget about the silly row."

"How long had you known Blake?" Helen asked.

"Since we were kids," James said. "We met at Eton. I was even best man at his wedding."

"What were you arguing about?" I asked.

"That doesn't matter now," James said. "The deal happened without me."

"Was it something to do with the vineyards?" I persisted. If Blake had shut James out of a profitable business deal that would give him an excellent motive for murder.

James shrugged. "We had an opportunity to buy extra land. It would have almost doubled the size of the vineyard. We both thought it was a good idea. I offered to go in with some money, take a cut from their business just like before. Blake turned me down. He said he didn't need my investment. In fact, he offered to buy me out of the whole thing."

"And you didn't want that?" I asked.

"Definitely not." James took a large slug of wine. "Firefly Vineyard is as much mine as it is his. I guess that's why he wanted to buy me out, make it a truly family business. But it wouldn't have been anything without my start-up capital. It didn't seem right that he wanted to stiff me on this deal."

"You wouldn't know if he was under any pressure from other investors?" I asked. "Maybe they didn't want another person coming in on the deal."

"What are you saying?" James lowered his glass. "He had other people he preferred to do business with?"

I picked at the napkin on my lap. "Not so much. But what if Blake got too stressed or anxious and couldn't find a solution?"

"Then he'd have come to me," James said. "We were friends."

"It can be hard to talk about things when you're under pressure. Did Blake ever mention finding things tricky? Or wanting a break from everything?"

"No! Well, nothing ever serious. He joked about starting again. Taking his old guitar and spending a month on a deserted island. But we all think like that at times."

"What if he was serious? What if he wanted out of this life permanently?"

"You're suggesting suicide?" James swept a hand across the table and knocked his knife to the floor.

I grabbed the knife and placed it back on the table. "You said he had something on his mind the night he died. And running a business is tricky. Maybe he didn't accept your investment because he was worried he might lose it."

"Nonsense." James finished his wine and refilled his glass. "Blake had an excellent business head on him, much better than me. And although I resented the fact he didn't want my money, I understood why he wouldn't take it. He thrived on the challenge the business presented. Firefly was not struggling. There were no problems he couldn't handle."

The sea bass arrived. I inhaled the rich lemon sauce before sampling some of the perfectly cooked fish. My theory of suicide didn't seem likely, but neither did the idea that a healthy adult male would fall over board and drown so close to the jetty.

"Blake had his stresses, but they had nothing to do with the business," James said.

"What were the stresses in his life?" I asked.

"Women. When is it anything else?"

"We're not all bad." Helen dabbed her mouth with her napkin, her fish already gone.

"I'm sure you're perfection." James grinned at her. "But he was having a few problems with Julianne. And then there was Honey."

"I heard a rumor they were more than friends," I said carefully.

"Their relationship was a strange one," James said. "She's a gorgeous girl, so I can see why Blake might be tempted, but I saw nothing going on between them. Perhaps they were being discreet, not wanting to rub Julianne's nose in it."

"You don't think they were having an affair?"

"Blake's not the type to cheat. We've had plenty of opportunities, two good-looking guys like us." He laughed and patted his paunch. "But the vibe I got off the two of them was more a friendly one. And he talked about wanting to mentor Honey and give her the opportunities she's never had. You don't talk like that when you're discussing your mistress."

I flashed a surprised look at Helen. Maybe Honey hadn't been Blake's mistress. She could really have been his assistant and he was helping her gain valuable experience so she could set up her own millinery.

"Julianne doesn't like Honey being around," I said. "That suggests she thinks something odd was going on between them."

"She can't stand the poor girl," James said. "And now Blake is gone, she bullies her. Has her working in the kitchen some nights. That's not what Blake would have wanted."

From what I was learning of Blake, he sounded like a decent guy, but he must've done something wrong to get himself shoved overboard.

We finished our food, and James grabbed the dessert menu. "I can never resist something sweet. Women, wine, and chocolate will be my downfalls. What a fabulous way to go."

"I'm the same," Helen said. "Well, apart from the women. And I'm more of a champagne girl. But dessert is my favorite part of every meal, even at breakfast."

James chuckled as he ran his finger down the menu. "You can never go wrong with chocolate brownie and ice cream."

I scanned the menu and selected a pecan tart with Amaretto cream. My thoughts shifted to the ghost dog who had remained at the house. "I hope you don't mind Flipper coming with us this evening."

"Not at all." James glanced at Flipper, who had curled himself next to my feet and been enjoying a few morsels from my plate. "He's well-behaved. I hardly noticed he was here."

"Does the family have any pets?"

"Not anymore. They had Dillon."

"Who's Dillon?" I asked.

"He was a black Labrador," James said. "The sweetest of dogs and so loyal."

"He's not around anymore?"

James lowered his dessert menu. "Ah. You didn't hear that part of the story?"

"Something happened to Dillon?" My stomach clenched and my hand reached for Flipper.

"That's the saddest part of this whole thing," James said. "Blake fell overboard, landed in the water, and Dillon jumped in to save him. They both drowned. Dillon died trying to save Blake."

Chapter 11

I stared open mouthed at James. "That's terrible."

"It is," James said. "He was such a lovely dog and devoted to Julianne and Blake. They got him when he was a puppy about ten years ago. He was always so well-behaved. Just like your dog."

"I always thought dogs were good swimmers," Helen said.

"Dillon was a good swimmer," James said. "But we assumed he got tired or wouldn't leave the water until he'd found Blake. It's terribly sad."

I exchanged a glance with Helen. At least now we knew who the ghost dog was.

We ordered our desserts, Helen choosing a triple chocolate sundae, and devoured them as we enjoyed the last of the sun and the view before it was time to leave.

Helen took great delight in cruising back to the house in James's Jaguar, while he sat in the back seat regaling me of his time at Eton and the fun he'd gotten up to with Blake.

"Our next trip out will be to the vineyard," James said, as we arrived back at the house. "I'll take you on your first day off. I always like showing beautiful women around the place. And you never know, I might get one of you to fall for me and leave your boyfriend for a life of wine and adventure in Cornwall."

Helen politely giggled, and I shook my head as I smiled at James. For all his flirtiness, he was an interesting guy. A little too fond of the booze, but he had fun as his top priority, and seemed determined to enjoy life.

We said goodnight to James, leaving him in the study to enjoy a large nightcap of whiskey, and returned to my bedroom.

I kicked off my shoes as Helen and Flipper settled themselves on the bed.

"So, we've discovered who our ghost dog is," Helen said.

"And we've also discovered another suspect," I said. "Despite James's good humor, it must have stung to be left out of a business deal like that. And he mentioned earlier that he'd won money on the horses. Perhaps his betting habit has gotten out of hand and he needed money. Money he would have gotten through this business deal Blake shut him out of."

"So, he thought he'd get rid of Blake and get his hands on the business?"

I scratched my head. "I'm not certain. It doesn't sound like he got anything after Blake died, though. Maybe he was thinking he could take over the business, run it for himself. Or buy Julianne out?"

"Then he ran into a problem when Marcus and Julianne started vying to be the boss." Helen stretched out across my bed. "You need to learn dog sign language. Dillon might have the answers for us since he was on the yacht the night Blake died. He would have seen if Blake's death was an accident or if someone shoved him overboard."

"Doggy sign language! You look into that and let me know how it goes."

Helen chuckled. "Even if I was fluent in doggy sign language, it would be no use to me, since I can't see the ghost dog."

I looked around the room and spotted a haze at the end of the bed. "Dillon's coming back. Poor Flipper won't be happy."

Dillon popped into view, his tail wagging, as he drifted onto the bed.

Helen shuddered and sat up. "Did he just climb over me?"

"He wants to get close to Flipper." I watched as Dillon turned in a circle and lay next to Flipper, who was already looking unhappy at his new companion's arrival.

Helen brushed imaginary dirt off her clothes. "Ask him what happened to Blake and see if he'll go fetch his owner."

My eyebrows shot up. "That's actually a good idea."

"I'm full of good ideas," she said. "Get Dillon to find Blake, bring him here, and we can figure out what happened to him. You could be right; this could all be a big misunderstanding and all we have is a confused dog who's lost his owner. Once we reunite them, they'll disappear and that will be it. End of the ghost mystery and we can get on with our jobs."

I patted the bed to get Dillon's attention. He raised his head and looked at me. "What do you think, boy? Fancy going to find your owner?"

Dillon tilted his head to one side, his ears raised.

"Find Blake," I said.

Flipper raised his head and a low grumble came from him.

I petted his head. "Don't worry. There's no need to get jealous. I'm just asking if Dillon can help us."

Flipper continued to grumble as he settled his head back on his paws.

"Maybe he's not growling about Dillon," Helen said. "Could be he's sensing Blake approaching."

"I can't feel anything." I looked carefully around the room, trying to pick up any sign of another ghost, but everything was peaceful and I wasn't getting the shivers.

"Dillon, go find Blake," I said. "Go find your master. He might need our help."

Dillon dragged himself to his feet and stared at me, his big dark eyes unblinking.

"He's not impressed with my suggestion," I said to Helen. "Go on, boy. Go find Blake."

Dillon grabbed hold of the sheets on my bed and yanked them off, making Helen yelp and Flipper jump to his feet and bark.

"Dillon, behave!" I grabbed the end of the sheet and pulled it away from him.

"I see what you mean." Helen helped me straighten the bedding. "Why is he getting so agitated about finding Blake? You think he'd be happy to find his owner."

"He could be confused." I watched Dillon pace across the floor. "He's trying to find Blake in the house and he's not here."

"Being confused isn't an excuse for messing with the bedding."

I ducked down, so I was the same level as Dillon. "Do you know what happened to Blake?"

Dillon's head lowered as he continued to pace.

"He's not here anymore. Blake doesn't live in this house. He's the same as you." I had no clue if Dillon understood what I was saying, but his pacing slowed and he sat down.

"Try to find him," I said. "We'd like to help him, and you, if we can."

Dillon's gaze shot to the bedroom door before he growled and vanished.

"What's wrong with him now?" I stood up.

"What's Dillon doing?" Helen asked.

"He just vanished." I tilted my head to one side, hearing footsteps rushing past the door. I ran to the door and opened it. Honey was hurrying away, a bag in her hand. "Honey, is everything okay?"

She turned toward me. There were tears on her cheeks. "No! Everything is awful."

Chapter 12

I gestured her toward me. "What's wrong?"

Honey sniffed, her gaze going to the stairs. "I need to leave."

"You can spare me five minutes," I said. "I'd like to help."

Slowly, she walked toward me, her shoulders slumped. She paused when she saw Helen and Flipper in the room. "I hope you don't mind me interrupting." Honey dabbed her nose with a handkerchief.

"Has something bad happened?" Helen asked.

"Oh, nothing really." Honey hovered in the doorway. "Well, actually everything. I'm not sure where to start."

"You're leaving?" Helen walked over, her gaze on the bag in Honey's hand.

"I have nowhere to go, but I can't stay here anymore." A sob hiccupped out of Honey's mouth.

"Let's talk about this over some hot chocolate." Helen marched out of the bedroom. "We can't have you leaving in the middle of the night if you've got nowhere to go."

Honey gave a small nod before following Helen. I walked beside her, Flipper at my heel. We didn't talk until we reached the kitchen.

Helen busied herself with making the hot chocolate, while I set out a plate of cookies, even though I was still stuffed from the dinner.

"So, what's wrong?" I sat next to Honey.

She sniffed again, her hands clasped in front of her, resting on the kitchen island. "Since Blake's gone, everything's gotten so much harder."

"You were fond of him?" Helen placed mini marshmallows on top of the hot chocolate.

"He was a good man," Honey said. "He treated me well. I felt so lucky to be here. Even though Julianne is so... difficult."

"She bullies you," I said.

Honey's eyebrows shot up. "You noticed."

"It's hard to miss," I said.

"Now Blake's gone, she's got me doing all sorts of things I hadn't expected," Honey said glumly.

"You were Blake's... assistant?" Helen passed around the hot chocolate and sat down.

"In a way," Honey said. "I saw it as a work experience position. I was trying all different aspects of the business to find out what I liked, see what I was good at, and what I needed training in. Blake supported that. He even said he'd help to finance any additional studying I needed."

"That was kind of him," I said. And not the thing most people did for their assistants. "How did you meet?"

"In the yacht club," Honey said. "I couldn't afford to be in there. You need to pay to be a member, but I slipped in the back door, ordered a lime and soda, and hung out with the rich people. It's silly, really."

"No, it's not," I said. "Sometimes, it's nice to get a glimpse of how the other half live. It's part of the reason we do these jobs."

Honey blushed and ducked her head. "And, I have to admit, it would be nice to find a rich boyfriend. I'm not a money grubber, but my mom's been sick and has missed several mortgage payments. We're getting desperate about where to find enough money to pay the bills. Blake overheard me asking for a job behind the bar."

"And offered you a place here?" I asked.

"That's right. We got chatting. He said I reminded him of someone he used to know. We got along well. At the end of the afternoon, he offered me this position. I couldn't believe my luck."

"When did the problems with Julianne start?" Helen asked. "I'm guessing she's the reason you're leaving."

"Pretty much," Honey said. "She was sharp with me almost straightaway. I did everything I could to get on her good side, but nothing made her happy. And whenever Blake's back was turned, she snapped at me. And I overheard her several times insisting Blake get rid of me."

"But he never agreed," I said. "That shows he thought you had potential."

"Blake was always stubborn," Honey said, a small smile crossing her face. "I think he partly kept me here because it annoyed Julianne. She wanted me gone and he didn't."

"Blake had a competitive side?" Maybe he'd picked a fight with the wrong person.

Honey nodded and then flinched back.

I looked down to see Flipper resting his head on her knee. "Don't worry about Flipper. He's friendly."

"I'm sure he's lovely. I'm nervous around dogs," Honey said. "I got bitten by a Jack Russell when I was a child."

"Flipper only bites on command," I said lightly.

Honey shot a nervous glance at Flipper. "I know it sounds weird, but I'm sure I keep glimpsing a dog around the house. Every now and again, I see a dog running along the hallway. No dogs live here anymore."

"Maybe it's a stray who snuck in," I suggested. Or, more likely, she was seeing the ghostly form of Dillon as he raced around the house, trying to figure out what had happened to him and his owner.

"It could be that," Honey said. "I'm always on edge. I never know when I will run into Julianne and she'll find some excuse to shout at me."

Flipper whined and stepped away from Honey. He could sense when he wouldn't win somebody around with his doggy charms.

"Are you sure you won't stay?" Helen asked. "If you talk to Julianne, tell her how you're feeling, she might realize she's being unfair on you."

"She doesn't care how I feel," Honey said. "She wants me out of here."

"Where will you go?" I asked.

"I've got enough money for a few nights in a hotel. After that, I'll have to figure out something else."

"Haven't you got any family you can stay with? You mentioned your mom," I said.

"I'm an only child, and Mom lives hundreds of miles away. Besides, I don't want to worry her when she's having her own troubles. She thinks I'm having a great time down here, learning how to be an entrepreneur. It would break her heart to know what's really going on and how much of a failure her daughter is. I should listen to Marcus, keep on husband hunting and use my *assets* to land a rich guy."

"I don't think that lifestyle will suit you," I said.

"Honestly, I'd be bored rigid." Honey shot me a smile. "I like to work for my money, and show I'm not some blonde airhead. I have a brain up here." She tapped the side of her head.

"You have my sympathy." Helen patted the back of Honey's hand. "We blonde bombshells must stick together. Sleep on it and don't go sneaking off in the night. Get a good night's rest, then consider your options in the morning."

"And we can help find you a new job," I said. "We have a great recruitment agency that found us these jobs. I'm sure they'll want someone like you on their books."

"You really think they'd help?" Honey's tear-stained face brightened.

"There's no harm in asking," I said. "You stay here for now. I'll get on to the agency first thing. Most of the positions are live in, so you'd solve your accommodation problem too."

"Thank you. That's kind of you." Honey finished her hot chocolate and stood. "Well, I guess I'm staying a bit longer."

"I'll let you know how I get on with the agency," I said.

We said our good nights and Honey left the kitchen, her step lighter and her bag swinging from her hand.

Helen looked over at me. "Don't forget she's a suspect in Blake's murder. You could be trying to get a job for a killer. The lovely Josie wouldn't be so perky with us after that."

"His *alleged* murder. And if Honey is involved, we can't let her leave," I said. "If she vanishes into the night, we'll never find her."

Helen ate a cookie. "So, we have Honey, Julianne, Marcus, and James as suspects. That's too many suspects and too many good motives for wanting to bump off poor Blake."

I stretched my arms over my head, the lateness of the hour catching up with me. "What we need is for Blake to turn up and point a finger at one of them. Help us solve this thing, so we're not left wondering what happened and why Dillon the dog is still around."

I hoped to get a good night's sleep, but with a head full of suspects and no clue who to target as a prime suspect, I doubted I'd get any.

Chapter 13

My teeth were chattering when I woke the next morning. I rolled over and gasped. Lying next to me was a gorgeous ghost. He had a bright, white smile, a strong jaw line, floppy dark hair, and bore a striking resemblance to Channing.

I sat up, self-conscious as I yanked the duvet around me. I recognized this ghost from the pictures I'd seen around the house. "You must be Blake Carlisle."

His grin widened. He nodded before tilting his head to one side.

"I'm Lorna Shadow. And I'm not sure it's appropriate for you to be in my bed, given this is the first time we've met."

Blake gave a silent laugh before floating up and sitting on the side of the bed.

I looked around for Flipper. He was usually great at alerting me when a ghost arrived. He was by the window, his tail tucked around him and a mournful expression on his face.

Next to him was Dillon, who jumped around and skipped on his paws, his attention fixed on Blake.

Blake patted his knee and Dillon launched himself toward him. As Blake stroked his head and ruffled his fur, it was easy to see he adored this dog. I sort of forgave him for sneaking into my bed because of that. He was a dog lover; he had to be a decent person.

"It's nice of you to make an appearance," I said. "I was beginning to think I'd have to get Dillon to show me what happened to you."

Blake looked around the room before shrugging.

"You're not happy to be back?"

He shook his head as he continued to pet Dillon.

"You don't have happy memories here?" I asked. "Or is it more to do with what happened to you on the yacht?"

Blake's fingers ran over the wedding ring on his hand. He ducked his head.

"Problems with Julianne?"

He nodded.

"Do you think she had anything to do with what happened to you? A jealous, vengeful wife is a dangerous thing."

He shrugged again before shaking his head.

"You still loved her?"

He nodded, before drifting around the room, Dillon following closely behind, his gaze fixed to Blake.

Flipper grumbled as he passed him. Blake paused and attempted to pet him, but Flipper shifted away. That was unlike him. He must be feeling off-color because of Dillon's presence.

"Can you show me what happened to you on the yacht?" I grabbed my dressing gown and pulled it on before getting out of bed.

Blake mimed being shoved.

"That's what happened to me," I said, more to myself than him. "When I was on the Orwell, someone pushed me over the side. I don't think it was a living someone. It wasn't you, was it?"

Blake's eyebrows shot up. He shook his head.

My phone buzzed and I grabbed it, seeing the call was from Zach.

"Good morning," Zach said. "How are things with your ghost dog?"

"So far, so strange," I said. "And I finally met his owner, just a few minutes ago."

"And is he being helpful?" Zach's tone was cautious.

"We've worked out he was pushed off the yacht. That's about it."

"Is he a friendly ghost?"

"He's friendly enough." I decided not to mention that I'd woken with him in my bed. Zach could hardly get jealous of a ghost, but that might be a little too friendly for his liking.

Blake and Dillon drifted around the room, not seeming in any hurry to figure out what happened to them.

Zach muttered a curse, and a door slammed.

"Is something wrong?" I asked.

"My favorite pair of shears are missing."

"You can't blame me for those vanishing," I said. "I'm hundreds of miles away."

"As if I would." His tone was teasing. "It's so weird. I'm sure I put them in our new garden shed, but I've searched everywhere. I figured I might have moved them to the cupboard under the stairs, but just looked. They're nowhere to be found. My last place to look was the lounge cabinets, but I checked the last one and nothing."

"Gunner's not been doing a bit of gardening and hasn't put them back in the right place?"

"Gunner is like you when it comes to the garden," Zach said. "He enjoys the view, but that's about it. I once gave him a job to remove the weeds from a flower bed and he pulled up everything. He claimed he wasn't sure what was a flower and what a weed was, so removed it all and started again."

"About Gunner," I said, "did you know he's in regular contact with Helen?"

"Not exactly. But he's always on his phone," Zach said. "And he's being a nightmare. He keeps pacing around and complaining about everything."

"Oh my goodness. He's missing Helen!"

"Yeah, but try getting him to admit that," Zach said. "I've asked him about her, but he says they're just friends."

"Helen told me their relationship is complicated."

"I wish they'd un-complicate things and get on with it," he said. "If he just admitted he was missing her, that would be a start."

"You should both come down here for the weekend," I said. "That might cheer him up."

"That's not a bad idea," Zach said. "And I am missing you a tiny bit. And Jessie's missing Flipper like mad. She keeps sitting by the front door and then giving me longing looks as if I'm going to magically bring Flipper through it."

"We can't have the dogs separated for long." Flipper could do with some time with his best friend. Having Dillon around wasn't suiting him. He needed something to look forward to.

"I'll speak to Gunner and see what he thinks," Zach said. "But it sounds like a plan."

I looked over to Dillon and Blake and saw them fading away. I gestured for them to stay where they were. We still had lots to figure out. "I'd better go."

"Don't let the ghosts mess you around."

"I don't think they'll be a problem. But there's a long list of suspects to work through."

"Work through that list carefully. Don't get yourself in trouble."

"I don't even know what that word means."

Zach grunted. "I'd better go hunt out these shears. Catch up with you later."

We said goodbye and I looked around for Blake, determined to start weeding out some of the suspects with his help, but he'd vanished, along with Dillon.

Chapter 14

It was the end of a long day of writing letters, answering emails and sorting through Julianne's admin.

She'd flitted in and out of the room most of the day, but never stayed long, so I was glad to have Flipper for company.

I'd just shut down the computer, when Julianne walked in, a pile of bills in her hand.

"I need to get these paid." She slapped the papers on the desk. "Honestly, some of these charges are ridiculous. I don't know what Blake was thinking when he paid them." She lifted a bill. "What is a 'discretionary service charge'?"

"I can double check them if you'd like me to," I said. "There may have been an error. You don't want to pay for something you never received."

Julianne slumped into her seat and let out a sigh. "That would be useful."

"I'll check through them all tomorrow."

She pulled out a file and handed it to me. "And take a look at these car lease agreements. I'm embarrassed to say Blake had a midlife crisis before he died. He signed contracts for two sports cars. I'll never use them. And now he's gone, they're sitting in the garage gathering dust. See if there's any way we can get out of the agreements without losing too much money."

"Not a problem," I said.

There was a knock on the door, and Marcus walked in. "Ladies! It's lovely to see you both. I hope you're both working hard, keeping the business going."

Julianne glared at him. "Well, it is my business to keep going."

Marcus looked at the file in my hands. His smile wavered before he grabbed it from me. "I can deal with the cars."

"That's not necessary." Julianne's eyebrows rose.

"It will be my pleasure," Marcus said. "If you're looking for a better deal, I'll negotiate something. It's a skill I excel in. Blake always said so."

"I want to send them back and stop being taken advantage of," Julianne said. "Can you make that happen?"

"Oh! The cars are important to the business, though." Marcus clutched the file to his chest. He clearly didn't want to get rid of his sporty rides anytime soon.

"We have a work van and our own private vehicles," Julianne said. "Those sports cars are an expense we don't need."

"We can afford it." Marcus's bottom lip jutted out, making him look about twelve.

"That's not the point," Julianne said. "We don't need them. And I've been checking through the accounts. Everything isn't quite as rosy as you make it is."

I shifted in my seat. I was interested to learn what Julianne meant. What was wrong with the accounts? I hadn't noticed anything odd, but I needed more time to scrutinize them.

"The business is flourishing." Marcus flapped a hand in the air. "But if it makes you happy, I shall contact the car company and see what deal they can do for us."

"Get them to take the cars away. That's the only deal I'm interested in," Julianne said.

Marcus's shoulders stiffened, but he nodded. "I'll see what I can do."

"If you can't do it, give the task back to Lorna," Julianne said.

"There's no need." Marcus tightened his grip on the folder. I'd have to pry it out of his cold, dead fingers before he let me take a look. "It will be my pleasure to do this."

Julianne shook her head. "I should never have allowed Blake to get the cars in the first place. Ever since he got them, things started to go wrong."

Marcus's eyes tightened. "The business isn't going wrong."

"It all looks good on paper, but the reality is different." Julianne rubbed her forehead. "I found bills that are three months overdue."

Marcus's gaze shot to the piles of paper in front of me. "That can't be right. It must be an oversight. Would you like me to take a look at the bills as well?"

"Lorna is going to do that," Julianne said.

Marcus's fingers inched toward the papers, but I placed my hand on top of them. Something was off here. Marcus was too keen to conceal what was going on with the business. He was hiding something.

"I'm taking a look at these tomorrow," I said.

A false smile slid across Marcus's face. "If you run into any difficulties, I'm always here to help."

I returned his smile with an equally false one. "Thanks for the offer. Hopefully, I can muddle through."

"Blake was so passionate about this business," Julianne said quietly. "But ever since Honey came on the scene, his attention shifted."

"He sounds like he was a dedicated mentor." I flinched as Julianne's expression harden.

"With his flashy cars and younger women, he was dedicated to the wrong things," she said.

"Blake loved this business," Marcus said. "And I know he loved you."

"Thanks for your opinion," Julianne said, her tone caustic. "But I know my husband. He wasn't being honest about a lot of things."

Marcus ducked his head. "I'll take my leave and look through this paperwork tonight. The cars will be gone before you know it."

Julianne watched him go without saying a word.

I sorted the bills into a neat pile and stood, not enjoying the tense atmosphere. "Same time tomorrow?"

Julianne jumped in her seat as if she'd forgotten I was even in the room. "Yes. Thank you for everything today. And sorry you've arrived when everything is in such a mess. I need to get this sorted as soon as possible and get rid of all unnecessary expense. Otherwise, I might have to let some staff go rather than hire new ones."

My eyebrows shot up. "I had no idea things were so bad."

"I can salvage it, I think." Julianne sat up straight. "Sorry. I didn't mean to burden you with that. You've only been here a few days and you're already unearthing our dark secrets. I promise you, it's not always like this. The business is doing well, but I am worried about its long-term success. It's one of the reasons you're here. I need your expertize to help me put everything in order and make sure we're working as efficiently as possible."

"I'll do everything I can to help," I said, "starting with these bills. Then I'll check through the accounts."

Julianne gave me a tired smile. "Thank you. Off you go. Go and get something to eat. We can sort through the bills tomorrow."

I hurried away from the office with Flipper, my stomach churning. Losing staff sounded terrible, and since Helen and I were so new, the chances were we'd be the first ones to go.

I walked into the kitchen and found Helen by the Aga, measuring spices into a pot.

"Can that wait?" I asked.

She turned and looked at me. "Sure. It won't be ready for another hour."

"I need some air. I've just had bad news."

Helen washed her hands and then hurried after Flipper and me out into the garden. "What's wrong?"

I took in a deep breath. "I think we might be able to lose our jobs."

Her eyes narrowed. "What have you done? Did Julianne catch you talking to yourself?"

"I haven't done anything." I shot her a glare. "But Julianne's just confessed the business isn't doing so well. She's talking about having to get rid of people. She must have discovered something really bad. A couple of days ago, she was planning to hire more staff, not fire them."

"What do you think the problem is?" Helen followed me onto the neatly manicured lawn, Flipper sniffing around our feet before bounding away.

"She's worried the books aren't balancing. And the business has unpaid debts," I said. "We don't want to lose our positions here."

"We definitely don't. We haven't had them a week," Helen said. "And we can't leave. I've got all those alterations to finish on Julianne's dresses."

"You won't be altering anything if Julianne can't afford to pay our wages." I watched Flipper running around the lawn, his tail up as he darted backward and forward. He was sensing something.

Dillon blinked into view. Flipper barked and raced away. But this time, he didn't seem unhappy about having Dillon around. Perhaps they were becoming friends, and he would stop feeling unwell around this ghost dog. It could be that confined spaces and Dillon didn't mix, and Flipper had picked up on that.

"Well, I guess it won't be too terrible if we have to go back home." Helen twisted her fingers together.

"You don't like it here?"

"Cornwall is lovely, and this house is great. But I miss... our place."

"Is it the house you miss or someone who lives in the house?"

"I'd just gotten my room how I like it," Helen said. "And then I had to leave."

"You're sure you're not missing Gunner?"

"Oh, I don't even think about him." Helen lied terribly. "And I'm sure he's not thinking about me. He's probably busy solving some horrible murder case with Matilda, while they eat her second-rate chocolate brownies and discuss the best month to get married."

I grinned. Helen was never one for understated. "Has he mentioned her anymore?"

"Only in passing," Helen said. "I pretended I hadn't heard him and changed the subject."

"As much as you want to go back to your room in our lovely house, we do need to figure out what happened to Blake and Dillon," I said. "And I haven't told you yet, but Blake finally appeared this morning in my bedroom."

"Did he have any useful insight into who shoved him off the yacht?"

"Only that he remembers someone did push him," I said. "His death wasn't accidental."

"But no idea who it was?"

"He was more interested in playing with Dillon," I said as we walked past some pale pink late summer roses. "But Julianne let slip something interesting just now. Blake was having a midlife crisis and leased some fancy cars. She even made mention of Honey and how she was a part of the problem."

"Blake tried to relive his youth by spending money he should be investing in the business, got himself a younger girlfriend, and then gets killed. It has to be Julianne. She's got the perfect motive," Helen said.

"She does seem the most obvious suspect," I said. "But until we've got proof, we keep an open mind. Marcus is still sniffing around, trying to lay claim to the business. And then there's James, who got shut out of a profitable business deal. He's fun to be around but could have a darker side."

"And Channing," Helen said. "We've not seen him around much, but maybe the brothers didn't get along. They could have been on the yacht and he decided to get rid of Blake."

"For what reason?"

"Blake annoyed Channing, so he shoved him overboard."

"You sometimes annoy me, but I don't kill you when I get the chance."

Helen huffed at me. "When do I ever annoy you?"

"When you're hiding your true feelings about Gunner."

"I'm hiding nothing," she said. "I've already told you it's complicated. I need to figure things out before I commit to anything."

"Just don't forget to invite me to the wedding when you have figured things out."

"You'll get an invitation," Helen said. "I want you to be my bridesmaid."

I grinned. "And you can be mine."

Helen's eyes gleamed. "Has Zach hinted he'll propose soon?"

I clasped my hands together. "I might have found a ring."

Helen let out a squeal so loud it hurt my ears. "Tell me everything!"

"I was looking for some clean underwear and found a ring box in Zach's sock drawer."

She swatted my arm. "And you've been keeping this from me. I need details. What's the ring like?"

"I didn't get a chance to look. Zach came in and almost caught me snooping."

"He's going to propose any day." Helen sighed. "How romantic. You must have a big wedding, with a five-tiered cake and a live band playing all night. And how about a choir singing as you walk up the aisle? Oh, do I get to pick my bridesmaid's dress? If so, I want teal. No, a scarlet red. Do you think Gunner will like that?"

"Hold on a second," I said, seeing the maniacal shine in Helen's eyes. "Zach hasn't even proposed yet. If he does, my wedding will be small and discreet. I don't want a live band or a choir. And as for the five-tiered cake, who can eat that much cake?"

"I've seen it in magazines. Each layer is a different type of cake, so everyone is happy. You have a chocolate sponge, fruit cake, vanilla sponge, carrot cake, and lemon."

I had to admit that sounded amazing. "I'll be happy with a small cake. A cake Zach and I will enjoy and everyone else has to put up with. Since it will be our wedding day, not theirs, that's the most important thing."

Helen pouted. "But you'll have a lovely dress? Please don't get all practical on me and decide for a pant suit you can wear again."

"Of course," I said, "but I only want close friends and family at the wedding. We'll have an intimate ceremony and a lovely meal somewhere. Then Zach, the dogs, and I can go off on a honeymoon. I want no stress when it comes to my wedding." As if that were ever possible. But I wanted to get married and remember it as fun and happy, not a haze of expensive fads I would never recall.

"I'll take care of everything for you," Helen said. "You tell me the theme, and I'll sort it all. I've always fancied myself as a wedding planner. Oh, and I can make your dress. You know I'd do an amazing job."

I laughed. "I was counting on you to make my dress."

Helen squealed again and hugged me. "This is going to be perfect. I can see you in a beautiful cream number. Off the shoulder if you don't think that's too daring. And a veil. You have to have a veil. I don't want to see you in a hat. It'll ruin your hair for the photos."

"I haven't thought about what I'm going to wear on my head," I said. "And just to be clear, Zach hasn't even proposed yet. Don't get ahead of yourself."

"But he will," Helen said. "He's got the ring! It's only a matter of time."

"So long as it doesn't go missing," I said.

Helen stopped walking and turned to me. "What do you mean?"

"Zach keeps complaining about things going missing in the house. His watch went missing, and he said on the phone today that his shears have vanished."

Helen frowned. "You know, I've been thinking about my eyelash curlers turning up in the cutlery drawer. It had slipped my mind, but I've also lost a lipstick, earrings, and a pair of pumps since we moved in. I thought I'd misplaced them or you'd borrowed them and forgotten to put them back. But if other things are going missing, it is a bit odd."

"It's nothing to do with me. And we live in a nice neighborhood. I can't imagine somebody sneaking in and taking our stuff."

"And it's such random stuff," Helen said. "If we had just a knicker thief, it would make sense. But why take Zach's tools and my lipstick?"

"It could just be that we're still getting used to our new house." A sliver of unease ran through me. This had happened to me before, my things being moved and disappearing. It hadn't been a living someone who had been moving things.

If we had a ghost in our home, Zach wouldn't be happy and would want to move. He'd been clear he didn't want ghosts living with us. But we couldn't move. I loved that place. We'd all worked so hard to make it a home.

Helen's phone rang. She pulled it out and squeaked. "It's Gunner. I'd better take this." She hurried away before I could say anything. The way those two were acting, she'd be the one getting married before me.

My thoughts shifted away from marriage as Flipper bounded around, dashing away from Dillon and barking at him.

I felt sorry for Dillon. His owner was dead and he'd died trying to save him. I wanted to help him and Blake figure out what happened.

They needed closure, and whoever killed them needed to be brought to justice. It was time to focus on this murder mystery.

Chapter 15

I hurried down the stairs the next morning, having overslept. I had no time for breakfast, so I ignored my protesting stomach and hurried to Julianne's office. As I reached the door, I heard raised voices, and paused outside.

"I know that's his watch you're wearing." It was Honey. She didn't sound happy.

"This was a gift." That was Channing. "You know how generous Blake could be. And he collected watches. The guy had dozens of them."

"That doesn't mean you get to take whatever you like. And I gave him that watch. It was a gift from me."

"You can have it back if you like," Channing said. "I didn't realize you'd given it to him. I guess it couldn't have meant too much to Blake if he gifted it to me."

"He'd never do such a thing."

"I'm only telling you what happened," Channing said.

"You're stealing a dead man's things! You've always been jealous of what he had."

I was surprised by how furious Honey sounded. The girl had a hidden backbone. I glanced along the hallway to make sure no one was watching me listen in and waited for more.

"I could accuse you of doing the same thing, coming in here and trying to get your hands on my brother's money," Channing said.

"It wasn't like that," Honey objected. "He was my friend. He looked after me."

"I can imagine what that involved."

"We were friends." There was a wobble in Honey's voice. Channing had pushed her too far.

I rested my hand on the doorknob, wondering whether to go in and break up the argument. If Channing had been stealing from Blake, maybe Blake had discovered what he was up to and threatened to tell the police. That would give Channing a motive for wanting him dead.

"He didn't employ you for your brains," Channing said. "We all know why you're really here. And you're still hanging around now he's gone, hoping to get the last few scraps before Julianne finally kicks you out."

"I have an employment contract. I have a right to be here. And I've done nothing wrong."

"Other than try to break up Blake's marriage."

"I was never going to do that," Honey said. "I like Julianne. If their marriage was in trouble, it had nothing to do with me."

"She hates you," Channing said.

"She'll like me a little more when I tell her what I've discovered," Honey said. "You've been stealing her husband's things. She's not going to like that. And Blake was annoyed with you too for not stepping up and getting involved in the business."

"You have no clue what you're talking about." Channing's tone grew cold. "I'd advise you to keep your mouth shut. Don't put dumb ideas into Julianne's head about my role in the business. I like things the way they are."

That was my cue to enter. I pushed the door open and discovered Channing standing toe to toe with Honey, who was backed up against the desk, a fearful look in her eyes.

"I'm sorry." I smiled at them. "Hope I'm not interrupting?" I looked at Channing and raised my eyebrows.

Channing backed away. "Of course not. We were just talking."

Honey glared at him. "Channing was leaving."

"I do have things I need to attend to." He made a show of checking the watch on his wrist before shooting her a sharp smile.

Honey huffed, but her jaw was wobbling.

"I'm glad you're here, Honey." I said. "I wanted to have a chat with you."

"Watch your back with that one," Channing said. "She's not to be trusted." He slammed the door as he left.

Honey let out a shaky sigh. "Thanks for that. I wasn't sure how to handle Channing."

"You were doing just fine. Sit down." I took hold of her arm and led her to a desk chair. "What's going on between you two?"

"I'm sure he's wearing a watch I gave Blake. I know Blake would never have given it to Channing. He loved that watch. He was so happy when he got it from me."

I bit my bottom lip. "Isn't it a bit unusual, giving your boss presents?"

Honey looked away. "He was kind to me. You buy friends presents."

She had a point, although I still wasn't sure just how close a friend she was to Blake. "So, Channing stole the watch?"

"He must have. Other things have gone missing too, and suddenly appeared in Channing's possession. Including an expensive car."

"Channing stole a car?"

"He's claiming he borrowed it. Two days after Blake died, Channing was driving around in one of Blake's convertibles. He said he was going to take it to the garage for a service, but it never came back. I've spotted him driving around the village several times."

"Does Julianne have anything to say about this?"

"She's too involved with the business to care," Honey said. "Maybe she thinks, because they were brothers, Channing deserves the car. And I'm worried he has designs on Blake's yacht. Although, why he'd want it after Blake died on there is a mystery. I get the shivers every time I step onto that thing, knowing what happened."

"He'll have a tough time trying to steal a yacht," I said.

Honey gave me a smile. "I bet he'll pull it off. Channing's a smooth talker. But Blake wanted him to grow up and be more active in the business. There was tension between them. That could be why Channing is taking things, petty revenge because they weren't getting on."

Since Honey was being so open, I decided to push my luck. "Can I ask you about Blake's death?"

She raised her eyebrows. "Of course, but I wasn't there when it happened."

"How certain are you that it was an accident?"

Honey's mouth opened, but nothing came out for several seconds. "That's what the police said. That's what everyone says."

"James doesn't," I said. "We had dinner together the other night. He isn't convinced that Blake fell."

Honey shut her mouth and tapped her fingers on her chin. "You think Channing had something to do with Blake's death?"

"I'm not sure who's involved," I said. "But it put doubt in my mind. I want to make sure nothing bad happened to him."

"Same here." Honey sat up straight. "Channing can be sweet and funny, but he's not so nice when he's been drinking. And I know he resented Blake for his success. He made snide comments about how much Blake spent on things and wouldn't it be nice if he got some of that money."

"What job does Channing have?"

"No job. He lives off his brother's income. Blake tried to get him to work in the vineyards, but he lasted a day, and ended up drunk in a store room. He gets a monthly amount paid into his account. Well, he did while Blake was alive. Julianne might have stopped that by now."

"Perhaps Channing wanted to get rid of his brother to get his hands on the money."

Honey's mouth formed a silent O as she stared at me. "I'm confused. Blake was murdered?"

If Honey was lying, she was very convincing. Her shock and surprise looked genuine.

Dillon appeared in the room, bounded over to Honey and laid his head on her feet. She shivered and shuffled away.

"You'd better keep quiet about my idea," I said, keeping a close eye on Dillon. "It might be nothing. Could be I've misunderstood what James meant."

"I hope you have. All this talk of murder is giving me the chills." Honey wrapped her arms around her middle. "I get what you're saying. People are benefiting from Blake's death. But I can't imagine anyone would kill him."

I offered up one last suspect. "What about Julianne?" I watched Honey's face carefully, but she was a picture of wide-eyed innocence.

"She's spiteful to me, but they had a rock solid pre-nup in case anything went wrong between them."

"Julianne gets to run the business," I said. "That's got to be worth something."

"It is," Honey said slowly. "And she still has this house. That's worth a lot of money."

"You know a lot about the family, considering you're an employee."

Honey's cheeks flushed. "Like I said, I really was friends with Blake. He could relax around me and talked freely about things that worried him."

"Like the business?"

"He was frustrated about the business because he couldn't run it independently. Did you know that James invested in the vineyard?"

"He mentioned it, but said he was more of a silent partner."

"A silent partner who made a lot of noise when he didn't get his weekly crate of wine sent to him."

"James was unhappy with Blake?"

"They were arguing about money, but I don't think there were any real problems." Honey swept her long hair over one shoulder. "Nothing worth killing over."

"What else was worrying Blake?"

"Family stuff. Personal matters." Honey clasped her hands in her lap. "I shouldn't gossip. Blake was a private man."

Dillon shot away from Honey's feet and raced around the room, making the temperature plummet. We both shivered this time.

I discreetly gestured at Dillon to stop running around before icicles formed on the end of my nose. "So, if you don't think James or Channing did anything to harm Blake, we're back to Julianne."

Honey blinked her large blue eyes at me. "Ten minutes ago, I hadn't thought anyone was involved in his death. Maybe Julianne was. She has a mean streak."

The office door slammed open. Julianne stood there, her hands jammed on her hips. "I'll show you mean."

Chapter 16

Julianne stomped into the office, her narrow-eyed glare pinned to Honey, who shrank back in her seat. "Just what are you accusing me of?"

Honey scrambled to her feet. "Nothing! I was just..." She looked over at me and pressed her lips together. "We were just talking."

I appreciated her not dropping me in it and felt a touch guilty that Julianne focused her anger on Honey.

"You were just gossiping about me," Julianne said. "Making me out to be a tyrant."

"You've always made it clear what you think of me," Honey said.

"Yet, you're still here."

"Not for much longer," Honey said. "Lorna's helping me find a new job. As soon as I've got one, I'll get out of your way. You won't ever see me again."

"Is this right?" Julianne's glare shifted to me, and I resisted the urge to shrink away just as Honey had done.

"I thought it might help Honey. She must have learnt useful skills in her time here. The agency I work with is always on the lookout for good staff."

"Make sure they don't put her with any families," Julianne said. "She'll only destroy them like she's done with this one."

"I haven't destroyed this family." Honey's hands fluttered over her chest. "I've always been nice to you."

"Only so you could get to my husband."

"He asked me to come and work here," Honey said. "*He* introduced himself to *me*."

"No doubt after you fluttered your eyelashes at him." Julianne sighed. "Let me make this easy on you. You're fired. Get out of here, right now. I have work to do with Lorna."

I opened my mouth to protest, but the rage in Julianne's eyes stopped anything from coming out.

Honey cast a fearful look at me before dashing out of the room. I could hear her sobbing as she ran away. My guilty feeling increased.

Julianne paced up and down the room several times, muttering under her breath, lost in her own thoughts.

Dillon, who had been watching the argument, began following Julianne, his gaze focused on her.

She slowed before heaving out another sigh. "Sorry you had to see that. But that girl had it coming."

"I'm not sure what went on before I arrived," I said cautiously, "but Honey seems like a nice person. And she's assured me she was only ever friends with your late husband."

"You shouldn't believe a word she says." Julianne sat at her desk. "I should have gotten rid of Honey the day Blake died. Ever since she arrived, he was distracted. And that's bad for everything. Bad for the business, bad for our relationship, and ultimately bad for Blake, since he's dead."

"Why was Blake so interested in Honey?"

"Do I have to spell it out for you? A gorgeous young woman, a man having a mid-life crisis, a wife too busy to notice things were going wrong." She gave another sigh.

"Do you know for sure?" I perched on the edge of my seat, ready to run if Julianne exploded with anger.

"Of course! Well, they were most likely having an affair. I never actually caught them together. But Blake bought her gifts, and she did the same for him on his birthday. That wasn't normal."

Since I'd interrogated Honey, it only seemed right I should do the same to Julianne. "Honey became possessive of your husband?"

"She was always a simpering fool around him," Julianne said. "Always trying to make him happy. It made me sick to see the way she fawned over him."

Now for the killer question. "And you're certain your husband's death was an accident?"

Julianne's breath shot out of her and her lips parted. "It was. What else could have happened?"

"If Honey became jealous and wanted to be more than Blake's mistress, and he refused her, do you think she would have done something about it?"

Julianne leaned forward in her seat, her gaze focused on me. "Has she said something to make you think that?"

"Nothing. But if Honey was with your husband, she might have become jealous."

"And wanted to remove me from the family home," Julianne said, her fingers tapping on the desk. "Take over and become the new Mrs. Carlisle?"

"Jealousy makes people do horrible things," I said. "I haven't got any proof that this happened, but if your husband's death wasn't an accident, there's a killer on the loose and you most likely know him or her." Or you are the killer, I silently thought, and I'd just revealed that I was poking around in a murder you committed.

Julianne stared into space for an uncomfortable length of time. "It can't be true."

Dillon moved to sit next to her, just as Blake appeared beside him. They both stared at Julianne.

"My husband's death was a tragic accident. Channing's right. Blake got drunk and fell over the side," she said.

Blake shook his head at this comment. He didn't agree with his wife about that theory.

"I hope I haven't upset you by mentioning this," I said. "I have an overactive imagination. But after the comments Channing made on our first night here, I did wonder if there was more to your husband's death than anyone realized."

She raised a hand. "I'm fine. I should thank you. It's nice to know someone is looking out for Blake, even though he's gone. And for all our problems, I did love him. I just wish he'd never brought Honey here. She's the real problem. If she had anything to do with his death, I will never forgive her."

The ice in those words made me shiver. I wouldn't want Julianne as an enemy.

Julianne seemed to withdraw after that comment, her hands clasped in her lap and her gaze fixed on nothing.

After sitting in silence for several minutes, I cleared my throat. "Well, I have bills to check and accounts to start looking at. What do you want me to start with first?"

"Oh! Well, both are important. Do whatever you want to first." Julianne rubbed her forehead as she stood. "I need a cup of tea and some time to think. I'll be back later."

I watched Julianne leave, her shoulders hitched and her head down. There was a woman carrying the weight of the world with her. She was coming to terms with her husband's death, seething over his alleged affair, running a business while fending off interference from

Marcus and James, and stopping a lazy brother-in-law from bleeding her dry.

I did feel sorry for her, but Julianne was still on my suspect list.

I looked over to where Blake and Dillon still stood. "We need another trip to your yacht, so we can finally figure out what happened to you."

Blake nodded before they both blinked out of sight.

The ghost hunting would have to wait a while. I had bills to pay and accounts to check. After all, dealing with ghostly problems did not pay the bills.

Chapter 17

It was late evening when I met Helen. I updated her about my conversations with Honey and Julianne as we drove to the marina to look around the Orwell and see if there were any clues we'd missed.

"You took a risk confronting Honey and Julianne, especially since it could be one of them who did it." Helen stopped the car in the marina car park and switched off the engine.

"It was worth it," I said. "Honey seems genuine in her fondness of Blake and she doesn't give off the angry mistress vibe."

"What about Julianne?"

"She gives off the harassed and angry widow vibe," I said. "But when I suggested Blake's death wasn't an accident, she was surprised. Actually, more like stunned."

"Are you ruling them both out?"

"Not yet," I said. "But we have other suspects to consider. Blake's brother, Marcus, or James could be the killer. The scorned woman angle might be the wrong one in this case. And after hearing how angry Channing was with Honey, maybe we should put him into the top slot for most likely killer."

"What are you hoping to find on the yacht?" Helen followed Flipper and me along the jetty toward the yacht.

"I'm not certain." I climbed on board and headed to the top deck. "But this is where Blake died, so he might give us a few clues as to what happened. I suggested he meet us here."

As I spoke his name, Blake blinked into view. He nodded at me before turning and looking at the water. He was closely followed by Dillon, who bounced around before racing over to Flipper.

"And, as if by magic, Blake is here," I said to Helen.

"I'll have a look around on the jetty," Helen said, her face pale. "Give you and Blake a chance to talk."

I smiled at her. "Don't go too far."

"I'll go as far as I need to, to stop the ground moving under my feet."

I joined Blake by the side of the yacht. "Is this the spot you fell over?"

He nodded, a sad expression on his face.

"Do you remember anything about what happened?"

He mimed being shoved over again.

"You didn't hear anything or smell anything, perfume maybe?" I asked. "Any hint of who pushed you over?" If he could remember a distinctive aftershave or perfume, it could jog his memory as to who was on board.

He shook his head and gave me an apologetic shrug.

"Don't worry. We'll figure this out," I said.

"Who are you talking to?"

I spun around and saw Channing halfway up the stairs, a drink in one hand and a curious smile on his face.

I shot a look at Blake. "Oh! Just myself. It's a bad habit of mine."

"That was quite a conversation you were having." Channing stepped onto the deck and looked around as if trying to see who else was here.

"It helps me get my thoughts in order when I speak them aloud."

"I should try that sometime." He took a large sip of wine. "May I offer you a glass?"

"No thanks," I said. "I didn't know anyone else was on board." I recalled Honey's words about Channing wanting the Orwell for himself.

"I like to come out here," Channing said. "I like being on the water."

"I didn't mean to intrude. I'd have announced myself before wandering around."

"Talking to yourself."

"Yes! Right! Talking to myself." My laughter sounded false.

Channing gestured to the side of the yacht. "You're standing in the place the police believe Blake fell over."

I took a step away and glanced at the railing. "It was a horrible way to die."

Channing walked over and leaned on the railing, peering into the water. Blake watched him the whole time.

"This sounds silly, but I miss Dillon more than I miss my own brother. I loved that dog," Channing said.

"I know what you mean," I said. "I'm the same with my dog." I looked over to where Flipper was hunched over, Dillon sitting next to him.

"They're only animals, so it shouldn't feel so painful to lose one, but it does," Channing said. "I remember him when he was a puppy. Even back then, he was well-behaved. And as he grew up, he learned all kinds of tricks. He could roll over and play dead. He would come when you called and was great at retrieving."

"It's sad how he died trying to save Blake," I said.

"The saddest," Channing said. "Shows he was loyal until the end."

"You mentioned that you weren't sure how Blake could have fallen in," I said. "What made you say that?"

"He was an experienced sailor," Channing said, his gaze remaining on the water. "He knew his way around this yacht. And he was a good swimmer. Even if he'd had a few drinks, he'd have known to get to the jetty and drag himself out."

"Unless he was injured." I shot a discreet look at Blake, who was still watching his brother.

"He did have a couple of bruises on him," Channing said. "The police assumed he hit something on the way down. Or there was something in the water and he landed on it."

"Was it a head injury? Perhaps he fell while on board and flipped over the side."

"Why the interest in my brother's death?" Channing gave me a curious glance. "Did you know him before you came to work here?"

"No. But the things I've heard since I got here suggest people are having doubts about his death."

Channing stood up straight. I suddenly realized how much taller he was than me. "What are you saying?"

"That his death wasn't an accident." I took a step back and heard Flipper growl as he picked up on my nerves.

"Someone killed him?" Channing snorted a laugh. "He was a great guy. Everyone loved my brother. I was the one who was the screw-up. There was never a bad word said about Blake. He was a golden boy."

"Why do you think you're a screw-up?"

"Its's always been that way," Channing said. "Blake was the one with the level head. Always coming up with good ideas about how to make money. Well, his ideas were usually good, until he decided to employ Honey. Then everything went wrong for him."

Blake moved closer. A chill ran through me as he passed by me and placed a hand on his brother's shoulder.

Channing shivered and took a gulp of wine. "I envied him. Everything came so easily to Blake. He always knew what he wanted. He met Julianne and they were married by the time they were twenty. It seemed stupidly young to me, but they were happy. Then he decided to run his own business, and the vineyard opportunity came up after Julianne's father died. He hasn't looked back since."

"And you resented him for that?"

"Resentment, envy, both similar feelings," Channing said. He shot me a sharp look. "Why do you care, anyway?"

I glanced at Blake, who still stood next to Channing. "I want to make sure that a decent guy didn't come to a sticky end."

Channing placed his wine glass down. "Oh, I get it. You think the younger brother had something to do with it. I let my envy get the better of me and got rid of Blake so I could take over the empire."

"I never said that." I shuffled another step toward the jetty. "Although, now you mention it, it is a good motive for getting rid of Blake."

"I wouldn't kill my only brother," Channing said. "I considered punching him a few times, especially when he got a bit smug about how wonderful his life was."

"Maybe you punched him on the night he died. Things might have gotten out of hand, especially if you'd been drinking." I glanced at the empty wine glass.

Channing reached forward and grabbed my arm. "You're seriously accusing me of murder?"

I tried to yank my arm out of his grip, but he held on tight as he dragged me to the edge of the yacht.

"My brother died down there," Channing said, pointing to the water. "He couldn't save himself that time. He wasn't so perfect that he couldn't get out of that particular mess."

My heart raced as I fought against Channing's strong grip. From the anger in his eyes, I could be Channing's next victim, and was determined that wasn't going to happen.

"What's going on?" Helen stood on the other side of the yacht. "Let Lorna go! You're scaring her."

"She thinks it's okay to accuse people of murder," Channing said, not taking his gaze from me. "She deserves to be scared."

Helen raced over and whacked Channing on the back. "Let her go!"

"Get away from me!" Channing turned and shoved Helen away, spinning me around as he did so, taking me away from the immediate danger of being thrown over the side.

I looked around for Flipper, wondering why he wasn't coming to help and groaned as I saw him throwing up on deck again.

Dillon stood next to Flipper, a concerned look on his face.

"Dillon! Help me!" I waved my hands at the ghost dog.

He jumped to his feet and bounded toward me, his focus on Channing. He leaped as he got close.

I pulled myself free from Channing's grip as they collided. Channing gave a startled yell as he plunged over board.

I watched in horror as Channing flew through the air, Dillon right behind him. They landed in the water with a huge splash.

"No way," I said as I swiped hair out of my eyes and stared at Channing as he floundered around, spluttering and cursing.

"Are you okay?" Helen grabbed my arm. "I thought you were going over again."

"Channing was just trying to scare me," I said. "But you won't believe this. I just saw Dillon push Channing into the sea. I think he's the killer! Dillon pushed Blake over board."

Chapter 18

Helen blinked at me several times. "The dog killed Blake?"

"He must have. I've just seen him barrel into Channing and shove him over. It makes sense now, what I felt on my back when I was pushed in. It didn't feel like human hands, but I couldn't work out what it was. Now, I know it was dog paws. Dillon jumped up and shoved me in the water, just like he did to Blake and now Channing."

"Where is Dillon now?"

"He went over with Channing," I said. "I'm sure he'll be back. And I need to thank him for saving me. Channing was getting mean."

"And Blake?"

"He was here." I looked around the deck. "But he's gone as well."

"We need to get out of here as well," Helen said. "Channing will think it was one of us who shoved him over. He's going to be angry when he gets out of the water."

I craned my head over the side of the yacht and saw Channing swimming around. I grabbed a float and flung it at him before we both climbed off the yacht.

Stopping by the jetty, I saw Channing holding onto the float and kicking his legs as he made his way toward the ladder.

He glared at me. "I wasn't really going to throw you over."

"You made a convincing show of wanting to do just that," I said.

"There was no need for your friend to shove me in." Channing glared at Helen.

"It's nothing less than you deserved," Helen said.

Channing glowered at her. "This suit is designer."

"It will make you think twice the next time you go around threatening women," Helen said.

He flung water at us. "At least help me get out."

"You can manage on your own," I said, before turning and hurrying away from the jetty with Helen and Flipper.

We ignored Channing's angry shouts as we disappeared back to the car. Only once we were inside, did I let out a breath. I still couldn't believe what I'd seen.

"Are you sure Channing had nothing to do with Blake's death?" Helen asked, as we shot away from the marina.

"As sure as I can be," I said. "And I saw what Dillon did. I waved my hand at him, and he shot into action."

"What do we do now?" Helen asked. "Even if Dillon was alive, we couldn't have him tried for killing Blake. It was just a horrible accident, after all."

"I guess it was," I said. "If that's the case, then why are Blake and Dillon still around? Why haven't they moved on if his death was accidental?"

I puzzled over this as we drove back to the house, Flipper grumbling in the back at having lost yet another meal because Dillon kept invading his personal space.

As soon as we got inside, we headed upstairs. Dillon and Blake were already waiting for us in my bedroom.

Blake was shaking his head as Dillon paced along beside him, his anxious gaze on his owner.

Helen pulled on a sweater. "From the temperature in the room, I'm guessing we've still got ghostly company?"

"They're both here and unhappy." I focused on Blake. "You don't think Dillon pushed you over the side of the yacht?"

Blake stopped pacing and stared down at Dillon. He petted Dillon's head and then looked at me.

"I understand if you're confused about this whole thing," I said. "You're not the only one. I thought someone in this family had killed you, not your dog."

Blake started making hand gestures at Dillon. Dillon's ears pricked up before he went through what looked like a practised routine. He sat, laid down, rolled on his side, rolled all the way over, and then jumped onto his back legs and put his front paws on Blake's shoulders.

"He's a well-trained dog," I said. "That doesn't help with what happened to you."

Flipper pawed at the bedroom door and began to whine.

"Poor Flipper." Helen opened the door for him. "He's having a rough time with this ghost mystery."

"He is. I've never seen him behave like this before," I said.

Flipper shot out the door.

I paused as I heard a high-pitched barking. "Or maybe his behavior has nothing to do with these ghosts." I followed after Flipper. "It sounds like he might be looking for a new friend."

We followed Flipper back down the stairs and into Julianne's office. She stood by her desk, a fluffy gray puppy cuddled to her chest.

She smiled when she saw us. "Oh, sorry. I didn't mean to disturb you. I know how late it is."

"Is that puppy yours?" I asked.

"Yes! I picked him up this evening." Julianne cuddled the puppy closer, his black eyes half-closed and his nose almost hidden in all the fluff.

"He's a cutie." Helen walked over and tickled the puppy under his chin.

"I'd forgotten how lovely it is to have a dog around," Julianne said. "When I saw you with Flipper, it reminded me how much I enjoy their company."

"I heard about what happened to your previous dog," I said.

"Yes, that was sad," Julianne said. "It still upsets me, thinking about how scared Dillon must have been." She placed the puppy on the floor. He bounded over to Flipper and grabbed the end of his tail.

"Don't do that!" Julianne chased after the puppy, who refused to let go of Flipper's tail.

Flipper tried to get away from the overenthusiastic pup as he chewed and sucked on his fur.

I picked the puppy off the floor and gently eased my fingers between his teeth, releasing Flipper's tail.

Flipper dashed to the other side of the room before tucking his tail tightly around him and fixing a stern glare on the puppy.

I passed the puppy back to Julianne, and she cooed over him. All was forgiven as soon as she was cuddling him again.

"Have you thought of a name?" Helen asked.

"Charlie," Julianne said. "It was my grandad's name. He loved dogs."

"It's a good name for a dog," I said.

"How did you come up with the name Flipper?" Julianne looked over to where Flipper was washing his tail. "It's unusual."

"He does a trick where he slaps his paws together when he wants a treat," Helen said. "He'll do anything for a piece of sausage."

"That's something I'll have to teach Charlie," Julianne said. "I want him to be as well-behaved as Dillon."

"Did you train Dillon?" I asked.

"I used to," Julianne said. "Well, I made use of Taylor's excellent services to start with."

"What sort of tricks could he do?"

"Just about anything." Julianne smiled at me. "Much like your dog, give him the right treat and he was happy to play along."

I shot a glance at Helen, an idea forming in my head, but she was still cooing over the puppy.

The office door was shoved open. Honey stood in the doorway, her angry glare fixed on Julianne. She held a piece of paper in her hand.

Julianne's eyes narrowed. "You're still here. I seem to remember I fired you."

"I've been checking my contract." Honey walked into the room. "And you need a genuine reason to get rid of me."

"How about your incompetence? That seems like the perfect reason to fire you."

"I'm more than capable of doing the work I'm given."

"How about the fact you and my husband were involved with each other?" Julianne asked. "I'd say you being involved in an adulterous affair is grounds for dismissal."

Honey's cheeks colored, but she held her ground. "My work here has always been of a high standard. And you've no proof of an affair. It wouldn't be right."

"At least you have one thing correct," Julianne said. "What you did with Blake was a disgrace."

"At least give me the wages I'm entitled to," Honey said.

"You'll get nothing more out of me," Julianne said. "Why don't you pawn the gifts my husband gave you?"

Blake blinked into view and stood between the two women, concern clear on his face.

They both shuddered in response to his presence but kept shooting angry glares at each other.

Blake moved to stand next to Honey and rested a hand on her shoulder.

I blinked in surprise and stared hard at them. They looked remarkably similar. Honey had the same straight nose and full lips as Blake. I took a couple of steps back, my mouth falling open as realization hit me.

"Is something wrong?" Helen whispered.

I nodded, still staring at Honey. "You weren't having an affair with Blake. He was your father."

Chapter 19

A stunned silence filled the room as I continued to stare at Honey. "You're Blake's daughter."

Honey's gaze went to the floor, but she nodded. "You're right. He was my father."

"That's not possible." Julianne grabbed the back of a chair. "I met Blake when we were young. I was his only serious girlfriend." Her gaze ran over Honey and her eyes widened.

"Did you know Blake was your father when you met at the yacht club?" I asked.

"I had an idea," Honey said. "I knew he lived around here and I knew his name. But he was the one to approach me that day. I don't know, perhaps he felt a connection between us or saw some of my mother in me."

"You cannot be his daughter." Julianne sank into the chair by her desk, still clutching Charlie the pup to her chest.

Blake moved to stand next to her and nodded slowly.

"I think she is," I said cautiously. "It makes sense now why they were so close. Blake wanted to get to know his daughter."

Julianne frowned, her attention on Honey. She passed Helen the puppy and grabbed a photograph off the desk before jumping up and holding it next to Honey.

She shrank away as if expecting Julianne to hit her. "I'm telling the truth."

"I'd know if Blake had a child. He always said he wasn't certain about children. We had talked about trying for a family next year. But this..." she waved her hand at Honey. "How is this real? How did Blake meet your mother?"

"Dad, I mean Blake, told me how he first met my mom," Honey said. "She's always had dreams of being a world-class singer, and started singing when she was only a kid."

Julianne gave an unladylike snort as her gaze ran over Honey again. "From the looks of things, she didn't do so well."

Blake frowned and shook his head, crossing his arms over his chest.

Honey glared at Julianne. "She did what she could to make things work for all of us. Mom met Blake one night in a bar when he was playing the guitar. He said it was love at first sight. They played together and fell in love."

"Blake hasn't played the guitar in years," Julianne said. "He kept saying he'd get rid of his collection. Although just before he died, he had mentioned wanting to play again. Now, I know why."

"He said the same to me," Honey said. "And he would have continued to play with my mom, but she fell pregnant with me and focused on raising me instead of pursuing her singing career."

"Your mom no longer sings?" I asked.

"She had to give it up," Honey said. "She used to sing anywhere, pubs, clubs, restaurants, wherever would have her. All the time, she was learning her craft and getting better. Back then, before the smoking ban came into place, she'd often spend hours singing her lungs out in a smoke-filled room. She's never smoked, but that's what the doctors believe gave her lung cancer."

Julianne's hard gaze softened a little. "I didn't know your mom was so ill."

"Why would you?" Honey said. "You never ask me anything, other than questions to find out what I've done wrong."

Julianne swallowed and a glimmer of shame appeared in her eyes. "I only do that because I thought you and my husband were... together."

"I know what you thought," Honey said. "Despite us both telling you nothing was going on, you didn't trust him or me."

"Why didn't Blake tell me about you?"

"He was going to, but was worried you'd leave him when you found out," Honey said. "He wasn't proud of this, but there was a brief period when he dated you and my mom at the same time."

Julianne's lips pressed together. "So much for true love. He cheated on me."

"He was young," Honey said, "and an attractive guy. Mom always said that about him. And he had mentioned you were very... persistent."

Julianne's glare returned. "So, what happened next?"

"It was just after you met that Mom got pregnant. They didn't know what to do. I wasn't planned, but Mom refused to get rid of me. She told Dad she didn't want to see him anymore. That wasn't true. She still loved him, but didn't want to tie him down at such a young age."

"She didn't want to stop him from pursuing his own dreams," Helen said with a sigh. "That was noble of her."

I flashed a quick look at Blake. His head was down, his expression sad. It must be hard to discover his first love so selflessly gave him up, and offered him the chance to do more with his life, without her and a baby holding him back.

"That's right," Honey said. "And Blake was a talented musician."

"He was a better businessman," Julianne said. "He was ambitious in whatever he did. I told him there was no money in music. He needed to focus his passions elsewhere."

"So he put his guitars away," I said.

Julianne shrugged. "It was for the best." Her gaze rested on Honey. "So, what did you do?"

Honey's eyes widened. "What do you mean?"

"You realized Blake was your father," Julianne said. "So you cashed in on the fact he was wealthy. You thought you'd come in here and take everything from me?"

"No! I simply wanted to know who my dad was," Honey said. "He'd been missing all my life. Mom wouldn't tell me anything about him until a year ago. Since then, I've been looking for him, and seeing if we could still have a relationship."

"He never looked for you," Julianne said sharply. "And he's never mentioned you. Doesn't that say something?"

"It says you're a controlling cow," Honey spat, "whose husband was too scared to be honest with her."

Julianne glowered at her. "At least his will makes sense now."

"What was in his will?" I asked.

"There was a strange paragraph in there about his children," Julianne said. "It said, if he had any children, they were to..." her words trailed off and she dipped her head.

"Did he leave me something?" Honey whispered.

Julianne lifted her head. "He did. This house."

Honey's mouth fell open. "I don't... I mean, really?"

Julianne scowled. "When the passage was read, I assumed he meant *our* children. We were considering being older parents, so I figured he was hedging his bets. If we didn't have children, the house would remain with me. I didn't know he was alluding to you." She jabbed a finger at Honey.

"I can't believe it." Honey stared around the room. "What am I going to do with a huge place like this?"

Blake smiled at Honey. He looked happy that he'd been able to do something good for his only child.

"You will not do anything with it," Julianne said. "Because I'm calling the police."

Honey took a step back. "You can't have me arrested for this."

"Not for this," Julianne said as she dialed the number. "What's to say you weren't involved in Blake's death? You came here looking for a handout. When he refused you, you got rid of him. You sneaked a look at the will and realized what you'd get once he was dead."

Blake shot toward me and waved his hands around, pointing at the phone and shaking his head.

"Hang on a second," I said. "Don't be too hasty about this. I don't think Honey would do that." Well, I had thought it for a while, but she wasn't the top of the suspect list anymore.

"Don't you get involved," Julianne snapped. "You're the one who put the idea in my head. You questioned me about whether my husband's death was an accident.

Now, it all makes sense. Honey turns up and Blake was murdered a few months later."

A sliver of guilt ran through me. She had a point. I had been snooping around and asking people about Blake's death.

"I didn't hurt him." Honey backed away toward the door, a fearful glint in her eyes.

"We will let the police decide that." The call connected and Julianne turned away. "Hello. I'd like to report a murder."

Honey's gaze shot to me. "I didn't do it."

"I'm sure you didn't," I said, catching hold of her arm to stop her from bolting in fear. "Explain everything to the police. It'll all be okay."

"What if they don't believe me?"

"They will," Helen said. "There's no proof that you were involved in Blake's death."

"I came here looking for my dad, that's all. I wasn't after money or anything else. I just wanted to know who the man was who'd meant my mom never found love again. I always figured he was somebody extraordinary."

"And I bet he was," I said. Although Honey looked genuinely shocked at the accusation, the more I considered it, the more I realized she did have a strong reason for killing Blake. Honey would have had access to Blake's papers and could have found a copy of the will. She'd admitted her mom was struggling and behind on the mortgage payments. This would solve everything. There might even have enough money to get her mom the latest cancer treatment. It must have been a temptation.

Julianne put the phone down. "The police will be here shortly. And they're very interested in talking to you." Her gaze settled on Honey.

"We should wait outside for them," I said to Honey, gesturing discreetly for Blake to follow us. "You look like you need some air."

Honey wobbled from side to side before nodding. "I need to get out of here and as far away from her as possible." She glared at Julianne before hurrying out the door.

I followed her as Helen stayed behind with Julianne.

"This is a nightmare," Honey gasped as we left the house. "She can't seriously think I killed my dad."

"Julianne's in shock," I said. "She's just found out she's got a stepdaughter."

"So she tries to have me locked up." Honey shook her head and stared back at the house. "All I wanted to know was where I was from and what my family was like."

Blake appeared and rested a hand on Honey's arm, making her shiver and step away.

"The police will want to know where you were when Blake died," I said. "Do you remember that night?"

"They've already asked me about that," Honey said. "They questioned us all after his death. I remember it well enough. I was here. Blake often went to the yacht on his own in the evening. He liked to use it for his thinking time. Things had been tense between him and Julianne and he used it as an escape."

"They were fighting about you?"

"They were fighting, but not just about me," Honey said. "But yes, he was worried about how he was going to tell her."

"If your mom had given him the choice, would he have stayed with her?" My question was aimed more at Blake than Honey.

Blake's eyes widened before he slowly nodded.

"Without a doubt," Honey said. "He loved my mom. He used to write her songs full of his devotion to her and how they'd spend their lives together. But she had to let him go. She didn't sing professionally for years after she had me. And even as I got older, she could only pick up poorly paid gigs. She sacrificed her career to raise me and sacrificed her relationship with my dad so he was free to do whatever he wanted. Mom always thought he'd be some super famous guitarist. Instead, Julianne forced him into this life."

"He didn't have to live this life," I said, glancing over at Blake. "Maybe he was happy doing this, instead?"

"I can't believe that," Honey said. "We shared a love for music. He was always introducing me to new bands from his childhood. Dad loved rock 'n' roll music. He even had a guitar on the yacht. He used to sneak it out and play when Julianne wasn't around. I'd never seen him happier than when he was making music."

Blake smiled again. He raised a hand to touch Honey's arm but then lowered it, his attention turning away from the house.

I looked up at the sound of tires crunching over gravel. A police car rolled to a stop outside the front of the house.

Honey took a step back, her hands going to her mouth. "What if they don't believe me? What if they charge me with Blake's murder?"

Blake shook his head and gestured for me to do something. I wasn't sure what he was expecting me to do. Now the police were here, it was out of my hands.

"They will if you're innocent," I said, not entirely convinced by my own words. "Tell them the truth. Hide nothing."

"But I've been left this house," Honey said, her voice quivering. "That's a great motive for killing my dad, a man I never knew existed until recently. They'll think the same as Julianne. That I came here for money and revenge."

"You were here on the night of his death. You can't be in two places at once."

"You don't understand. Nobody saw me." Honey watched as two police officers climbed out of the car. "I was alone in my room that night."

"Are you sure no one can vouch for you?" Suddenly, things didn't look so good for Honey. She could easily have snuck out of the house, gone to the marina and killed Blake.

"I keep to myself." Honey's bottom lip wobbled. "It's easier to keep my head down and stay out of the way."

One of the police officers, a tall broad man with a crooked nose and brown eyes, stopped beside us. "I'm looking for Mrs. Julianne Carlisle?"

"She's in the house," I said.

"And you are?" the police officer asked, his sharp gaze running over me.

"Lorna Shadow, her personal assistant."

The police officer's gaze went to Honey and he raised his eyebrows.

"I'm Honey Partridge," she whispered.

"Don't go anywhere, Miss Partridge," the police officer said. "You stay here," he said to his colleague. "I'll go in and talk to Mrs. Carlisle."

I tightened my grip on Honey's arm. I hoped she could prove her innocence. But right now, things didn't look too good for her.

Chapter 20

It was late that same evening, and I couldn't sleep. Honey had gone in for questioning by the police. Julianne was in bed with a headache, keeping Charlie the pup with her, and Blake had vanished, again.

I was torn up with indecision about Honey's involvement in Blake's murder. She had the perfect motive but had been terrified when the police took her away.

Sighing, I climbed out of bed, wrapped myself in a dressing gown, and headed downstairs to the kitchen, Flipper by my side. Maybe some sugar and chocolate would help clear my thoughts.

I'd just finished making myself some cocoa, when Helen's head appeared around the kitchen door.

"I thought I heard you go past my door." Her eyes landed on the cocoa. "Got any spare going for me?" She came into the kitchen, wearing a bright pink dressing gown, and sat at the table.

"Sure. Although it won't be as good as yours." Helen had a secret way of whipping the cocoa until it was creamy and full of delicious sugary froth.

I made more cocoa and then joined her at the table.

"Thinking about Honey?" Helen asked.

"I can't decide if she's guilty," I said. "And I hate to think of her stuck at the police station being interrogated."

"Surrounded by all those gorgeous policemen."

I smacked her arm. "They don't all look like Gunner."

There was a quiet tap on the kitchen door. James appeared, his shirt disheveled and a glass of whiskey in one hand. I checked the wall clock and saw it was past midnight.

"I hope you don't mind me joining you, ladies." James wobbled his way to the table and sat down. "I saw Helen come in and wanted to catch up on all the news."

"Have you been having a fun night?" I asked him.

"Yes. Bit too much fun, actually." He ran a hand down his face.

"I'll make you some coffee," Helen said.

"If you put whiskey in it, I'll say yes," James said, staring at her with bleary eyes.

"Maybe you've had enough for one night," I said, my gaze on the whiskey glass.

He shrugged. "Channing's been telling me about what happened with Honey. I didn't figure her as the sort of girl to commit a murder."

"That's what I'm trying to figure out," I said. "Do you know Honey well?"

"No. She kept to herself," James said. "She was often hanging around when Blake did business. He said he liked her being there and she was getting hands-on experience of how to run things. I never could figure out their relationship. Now, it all makes sense. Who'd have thought it, my business partner had a secret love child. It's all very scandalous."

"Honey won't appreciate being thought of as a scandal," I said.

"I bet she won't." James accepted the coffee from Helen and sniffed it gingerly. "Are you sure you put whiskey in this?"

"Just drink it," Helen said as she sat back down.

James took a sip and wrinkled his nose before putting down the mug. "Well, at least we now know what happened to Blake. I always thought his death was a bit odd."

"We don't know for certain it was Honey," I said. "The police are only questioning her for now."

"It's a terrible business. What we need is something to cheer ourselves up," James said, his fingers tapping the edge of the table. "Something to bring the brightness back after this shock."

"What do you have in mind?" Helen asked.

"A trip to the vineyard," James said. "I promised I'd take you both. Now's the perfect time. Julianne won't be up to much while she sorts out this mess, which leaves you free to come out with me."

"Our day off isn't until the weekend," I said. "She might want us around."

"Julianne is leaving for a couple of days," James said. "I heard her making the arrangements on the phone. She won't be around to care what the two of you do. Take your day off early. I'll treat you to some fun at the vineyard. All the wine you can dream of."

"I could bring along a cheese board and some fresh bread," Helen said, her eyes bright at the thought of delicious food and wine.

"Now you're talking," James said. "What do you think, Lorna? Time to get away from all this misery and enjoy ourselves? Blake wouldn't want us moping around. He was always the first to open a bottle of wine and have a laugh."

I chewed on my bottom lip. I couldn't do anything to help Honey while she was being questioned. "A day out would be nice. Okay. I'm in."

"That's a good girl," James said.

"We can head off early," Helen said. "Make a day of it."

James's nose wrinkled again. "Why don't I meet you outside at noon? I'm not an early riser."

We would miss half the day by the time James surfaced. But it would give me time to investigate the accounts with no distraction, something I'd been meaning to do. "It's a date."

James clapped his hands together and picked up his mug of coffee. "Excellent news. I'll see you ladies tomorrow. Don't stay up too late." He staggered out of the kitchen, looking like he was heading toward the lounge to continue his drinking session.

I let out a sigh and took a sip of my cocoa.

"So it's all over," Helen said.

I shrugged. "I guess so. Honey's being questioned. She has no alibi and a good motive."

"And the ghosts?"

"They're not around."

"So, no more mystery to solve."

Something niggled in the back of my mind. I still wasn't convinced. "I'd like to see Blake one more time, see if I can jog his memory about Honey's involvement in his death, just to be certain it was her."

"If he doesn't come back, it proves she did it," Helen said. "Maybe he remembered she was there the night he died and that was all he needed. Blake's gone now his killer has been caught."

It was a convincing argument. Honey was in the frame for Blake's murder. Maybe that really was it, and I'd been letting my budding friendship with her cloud my judgment.

"Come on. We need to get some rest. We've got a busy day of wine slurping to look forward to."

I put on my sunglasses and smiled up into the brilliant blue sky. It was a perfect day to go to a vineyard.

I'd spent the morning scouring the accounts, checking the bills, and making sure everything was in order with the business.

I'd found a few things that could be trimmed and a staff member who was receiving a larger salary than most. There was also a business receiving a large payment every month, J.M. Smithe, but I couldn't find out why they were being paid. They weren't listed in any company directory. I needed to find out more about them from Julianne. It looked like they'd received this payment every month for years, so they must be a regular supplier of something.

Helen hurried out the front door of the house, a picnic hamper over one arm. "I've got everything. I've packed the cheeses in a cool box, and there's freshly baked bread, olives and then fruit for dessert." She wrinkled her nose. "I'd have liked something that was actually a dessert, but chocolate will melt in this heat."

"Fruit will be lovely," I said.

"This is just what we need after everything that's happened," Helen said. "A fun day out, with no ghosts or mysteries to solve."

I looked around the garden, half expecting Blake or Dillon to appear. But ever since Honey had been arrested, there was no sign of them. Perhaps Helen was right. Blake's murderer had been uncovered so there was no reason for them to hang around.

"From your silence, I'm guessing you're still not convinced it was Honey?"

"She seemed so shocked," I said. "And I was beginning to like her."

"And you're such a good judge of character." Helen nudged me with her hip. "After all, you picked me to be your best friend."

"A decision you remind me of regularly." I grinned at her. "Maybe it's nothing. Honey is guilty and the police will find the evidence they need."

"But until they find rock solid evidence, you will keep on snooping?"

"I won't snoop," I said. "But if information comes my way that helps clear Honey's name, I'll look into it. We can't have the wrong person going to prison for Blake's death."

James's Jaguar cruised around the side of the house and stopped in front of us. He hopped out and took the picnic hamper from Helen. "Good afternoon, ladies. Are you ready to sample some wine?"

"We can't wait." Helen hopped into the back seat alongside Flipper and me.

James drove out of the driveway. "Have you both gotten over the shock of yesterday yet?"

"Just about," I said, "but I hope Honey is okay."

"I always had her down as a sweet girl," James said. "She was never any trouble and always easy on the eye. I'll miss that."

I shook my head at Helen. "Looking good is an important quality."

James chortled. "What can I say? I'm a man. I like to look at women. There's no harm in that."

"Have you seen Julianne this morning?" I asked. "I looked around but couldn't find her. I wanted to double check some details in the accounts."

"She planned to leave at dawn," James said. "Needed to get away from all of this. I can't say I blame her."

I nodded. Julianne had been stunned by the revelation Honey was Blake's daughter. But what if that had been a ruse? What if she knew all along and had set up Honey? It would be the perfect act of revenge. Get rid of her husband's secret love child, get rid of the husband, and then reap the rewards.

Sitting back in my seat, I sighed. I could come up with these wild theories all day, but with no proof, it was all for nothing.

Flipper rested his head on my knee and looked up at me. I stroked his head. I needed to stop worrying and enjoy myself. Sunshine, good food, and wine would make things better.

We arrived at Firefly Vineyard twenty minutes later, the sun still glorious overhead.

James opened the back door of the car and extended his hand to us. "Welcome to The Pigsty."

I looked around and saw acres of vines spread before us. I expected to be overwhelmed by the scent of ripe fruit, but all I got was a tang of overly ripe grapes. It was a sweet, cloying smell on the breeze. "This used to be a farm?"

"That's right." James collected the picnic hamper and strode ahead of us. "An enormous pig farm. Let me tell you, the place stank the first time we looked at it. But Blake had the vision to see it could be so much more. When they arrived to take over the existing business, Blake knew this place would be perfect to expand into. And he had a soft spot for pigs and decided they deserved a better life than ending up in someone's bacon roll."

"What happened to the pigs?" I asked.

"They were sent to a rescue center," James said. "And he kept a few. Gave them all names. He loved his animals whether they had fur or trotters."

"It's beautiful here," Helen said.

"I like it," James said. "Fifty acres, all producing top-quality wine. Come on, we'll take a walk around. Then I'll set up our own private tasting experience."

I ambled along as James explained how the grapes were chosen, cultivated, and then picked when ripe, before being processed and bottled for sale.

Flipper walked along beside me, happy to explore his new surroundings. Now he was away from Dillon, he was back to his old self. I was convinced Dillon's ghostly presence was the cause of his sickness. Still, a quick trip to the vet wouldn't do any harm, just to make sure everything was fine.

"Who are they?" I pointed to a group of people in the distance.

"Probably a tour group," James said as his gaze followed my finger. "We run them in the summer. People love to come and have a look around and sample the wine. It's also an excellent way to sell a few bottles. It's delicious stuff."

"When do we get to try the wine?" Helen asked.

"Well, beautiful lady, you set up the picnic out here. I'll go and snag us a few bottles. Wine tastes even better outside in the sunshine."

Helen nodded, and we followed James to a large wooden barn, the double doors thrown open and a strong scent of fermenting grapes drifting out.

"There's a good spot around the corner." James handed Helen the picnic basket. "Get out the food. I'll be back in a jiffy."

We wandered around the side of the barn. I could hear murmurs from the visitors inside and the chink of glasses.

Helen set the blanket in a shady spot and took out the food, arranging it neatly. "Isn't this lovely? Just what we needed."

"You're right. This is nice." I felt relaxed now we were here and had barely thought about Honey and her situation. She'd be fine. The police knew what they were doing. If she was innocent, they'd let her go. And if she wasn't, well, that would be a shame, but at least Blake's murder was solved.

I sat on the blanket, and Flipper joined me, his nose pointing straight at the food, just in case any escaped and happened to fall into his mouth.

"Don't worry. You'll get some," I said. I'd packed him a special treat, so he wouldn't keep pestering us for food.

James strolled around the corner a moment later, two bottles of wine tucked under his armpits and two in his hands. Three long-stemmed glasses hung from his fingers.

"We're going to drink all that?" I wouldn't be able to stand up if we did. And there'd be no way I'd get in a car after James had downed that wine.

"These are just for starters," James said, grinning as he set down the glasses and wine. "And you don't have to drink a whole bottle if you don't want to. We're only sampling. But you can pick your favorite and I'll get us a bottle of that." He shrugged off his linen jacket and squeezed onto the blanket before uncorking the first bottle.

"What's this one?" Helen asked, as James passed around a small measure of white wine.

"Firefly Vineyard has five different varieties. Each one has the word pig in the name, in honor of our former residents. This is the *Clever Pig Chardonnay*. It's a cheeky little number, with a crisp flavor and a hint of lemon and grass."

I raised my eyebrows as I sniffed the wine. I was no wine connoisseur and couldn't pick up any hints of lemon or grass. But I liked Blake naming the wine after the animals he'd saved. I took a sip. It tasted like white wine. It was nice enough. I could drink a glass or two without complaint.

"This is lovely," Helen said, after she'd taken a sip. "I might have to get a bottle of this."

"There's plenty of the stuff back at the house if you ask Julianne nicely enough," James said. "She might need someone to talk to over a glass of wine after everything that's happened. Honey is a big problem for Julianne. I bet she's fretting about what to do, worried the villagers are gossiping."

"It's not just Honey that's a problem," I said, wondering how much James knew about Julianne's financial concerns. "She was talking about cutting business overheads, even letting go of staff."

James's eyes widened. "First I've heard of it."

"I only know because she asked me to look over the books. Julianne was worried there might be unnecessary expenses going out."

"And are there?"

My fingers tightened around the wine glass. "There are a few anomalies, one in particular. Do you know anything about a company called J.M. Smithe?"

James sat up straight. "I'm not familiar with that name. Is it a local firm?"

"I'm not sure. But they get paid regularly. I can't figure out what for."

"What amount are we talking about?"

"Five thousand a month."

His eyebrows shot up. "Blimey. What do they do to earn that? It's not a wine merchant. I'd know them. What does Julianne think about it?"

"I haven't had a chance to ask her," I said. "I only found the amounts this morning."

"I'd like to help." James scratched a hand through his hair, "but accounting isn't my thing. I find the money, make the investment, and leave things to flourish. But if someone is skimming money off this business, then we need to get it sorted. We can't have anyone taking my profits."

"Any idea who might want an extra cut?" I asked. "Any member of staff been unhappy recently?"

"Again, not my sort of thing," James said. "But a smart girl like you will figure things out. Julianne's already said how pleased she is with your work."

"I hope she's happy with the work I've been doing as well," Helen said as she finished her wine.

"I'm sure she's thrilled with you both." James smiled at Helen. "Are you ready to try the next bottle?"

"Absolutely." Helen grinned, her cheeks already pink from the wine.

We spent the next half an hour sampling wine and eating cheese and bread. The accounting issue kept playing on my mind, despite how hard I tried to ignore it. I doubted Honey would have been skimming off the books, but she was a smart young woman, no matter what Julianne and Marcus said about her. Maybe Blake had taught her too well. That would be another thing the police would figure out. If Honey was stealing money, Blake might have caught her and she'd panicked. It was just another nail in her coffin, another reason for wanting him dead. Another reason for killing him.

We were about to sample our third bottle. I felt pleasantly relaxed and a little tipsy, when Flipper shot to his feet, abandoning his dog chew.

I reached for his collar, but before I could stop him, he'd dashed away through the vineyard.

"What's up with him?" Helen cut a large chunk of cheddar cheese and placed it on a slice of bread.

I clambered to my feet and watched Flipper race through the vines. "I'm not sure, but I better go get him. He's probably spotted a rabbit or another dog and is off to make friends."

"Don't be too long, or we'll drink all the wine," Helen called.

I gave her a wave as I called to Flipper, but he ignored me. I saw him racing toward a fence, which he leaped over without pausing.

Increasing my stride, I stopped by the fence. There was nothing in the field other than recently mown grass, so I didn't have to worry about Flipper racing through crops and getting shot by an angry farmer.

As I looked for a way to get over the fence while maintaining my dignity, I heard barking. I looked up to see a husky dash across the field, grab something, and then turn and race back the way it had come.

The dog looked familiar. As I hauled myself over the fence, I spotted a person. From this distance, I couldn't be certain, but it looked like Taylor, the dog trainer.

I watched as the husky sat at her feet and dropped whatever was in its mouth. She petted his head and then fed him a treat before sending him off to retrieve something else.

When the dog returned, she started him on a series of commands, including sitting, laying down, and then jumping up. He did everything she asked. Taylor was good at her job. I'd have to get her to teach me how to make Flipper stop running away whenever he found something interesting.

She looked up and waved as she saw me approach. Flipper was now sitting by her feet, his tail tucked neatly around him. He'd do anything for a treat. No doubt Taylor had a stash of goodies on her.

"Sorry about Flipper," I said as I reached her. "He must have smelt your dog and come to investigate."

"I was using a dog whistle," Taylor said. "Perhaps that's what he heard. Some dogs react to it and some completely ignore it. I also use hand gestures when teaching dogs new tricks."

"I've never used a whistle with him," I said. "But if it brings him to heel like this, then I'm buying one today."

Taylor laughed and pushed her curls off her face. "I didn't know you were here."

"James is giving us a tour," I said. "Julianne is having a couple of days away, so I've got the day off."

"Oh, yes." Taylor looked down at the dogs. "The whole village is talking about what happened. Honey getting arrested and all that."

"She hasn't been formally charged. But Julianne's convinced Honey's involved with Blake's death." Thanks to a little prodding from me, something I still felt guilty about.

"Do you think she's innocent?"

"I honestly don't know," I said. "I was just getting to know her when they arrested her."

"The police will sort it out," Taylor said. "And if she did anything to hurt Blake, then she deserves to go to prison. He was a nice guy."

"You trained his old dog, Dillon?"

"That's right. Up until he died, he used to come to one-to-one classes once a week. I've been running this business for fifteen years and was around when they got Dillon as a puppy. And I hope to train Charlie, as well. Have you met him yet?"

"Yesterday," I said. "He's a cutie."

"He's perfect. And Julianne will need a companion, given everything that's happened," Taylor said. "I'll drop by in a few days and see if she needs a hand with Charlie. He will take her mind off everything. When you have a dog in your life, everything seems brighter."

I smiled and nodded. She was right there. Until I'd gotten Flipper, I always felt there was something missing in my life. "What are you doing out here?"

"Julianne lets me use this field for training," Taylor said. "I tried to pay her to rent it, but she said it's just going to waste. It's the wrong soil type to grow grapes. So, I come here most days and train the dogs. Sometimes, I use it to give Brutus a good run around. He's got a lot of energy. And it's nice out here. I like the peace and quiet."

"I must come out here with Flipper. You can show us a few tricks," I said.

"He seems like a well-behaved dog." She petted his head, and he gave her a doggy smile.

"When he wants to be," I said, with a wry grin. "But he has a mind of his own."

"That's the best kind of dog," Taylor said. "I like the ones with character. You know when they're coming to your command that they're doing it because they respect you, not because you've forced them. Positive reinforcement is the best way to go. You can get them to do anything when they know there's a bit of liver sausage at the end of it."

I grinned. Taylor certainly knew her animals. "We could meet up next week for a walk and a training session?"

"You'll find me here almost every day," Taylor said as she pulled out a card from her pocket and handed it to me. "Send me a text when you want to meet."

"That sounds great," I said. "Well, we'd better get back to our wine tasting. I'm worried Helen will drink everything and I'll have to carry her to the car."

Taylor raised a hand as we walked away before sending Brutus off for another retrieval.

Flipper jumped over the fence, and I hauled myself over. I turned to look back at Taylor and Brutus and paused. Someone else had joined her.

I squinted. It looked like Marcus. What was he doing with Taylor?

I watched as Brutus ran toward them. He dropped the ball he held in his mouth. Marcus made a gesture with his hands and Brutus backed away and then ran straight at Taylor and jumped at her.

My eyes widened as I heard them laughing. Taylor got to her feet and brushed herself down.

Marcus repeated the movement and Brutus did the same thing before sitting and barking until Taylor gave him a treat.

I backed away from the fence, my heart thudding. The theory about Blake being pushed overboard was correct. But it wasn't Honey who'd pushed him over.

I'd been right the first time. It was Dillon all along, but he didn't do it by accident. He'd been trained.

I felt sick as I ran through the vines. For whatever reason, Taylor and Marcus had trained Dillon to kill Blake.

Chapter 21

I found Helen and James giggling like schoolchildren as they finished another bottle of wine.

"I've just seen Taylor training her dog," I said, raising my eyebrows at Helen.

"That's nice," Helen said.

"She does that," James said. "Uses the field next door to train the dogs."

I tried to shove my muddled thoughts into order as I caught my breath. Why would Taylor train Dillon to push Blake off the yacht, and how was Marcus involved?

Helen gave me a quizzical look as I continued to stand in front of her. "Is everything okay? Want to try some more wine?"

I scraped my hair off my face. "I'm not sure. And no to the wine." I turned to James. "Do you know if Taylor and Marcus are an item?"

"Marcus Patel dating Taylor?" James laughed. "He's not her type. She likes the outdoorsy sort, lumberjack shirts, beards, and walking boots. I've never seen Marcus out of a suit and tie."

"Why do you ask?" Helen sat up straight, finally seeming to sense something was wrong.

"You interested in Marcus?" James asked. "I thought you said you weren't available."

"I'm not." I needed time to work through what I'd seen. "We should go. We don't want to get back too late in case Julianne returns."

"Don't worry about her," James said. "She'll be away for at least a day."

"Even so, we need to get back." I shot Helen a meaningful look, trying to get her on my side, but she was busy picking over the last bits of cheese.

"I've got a couple more bottles for you to try yet," James said. "We've got the *Noisy Pig* and the *Angry Boar* to sample."

"Let's try them back at the house," I said, searching around for a convincing argument to get them to leave the wine and cheese. "Helen, you'd better not stay out any longer. You don't want to get sunburnt."

Helen frowned and checked her arms. "I'm not burning."

"Even so, you can never be too careful." I grabbed her arm and hauled her to her feet, the time for subtlety over. "And I'm driving."

"I'll be fine to drive." James clambered to his feet and wobbled to one side.

"Don't even try to argue about this," I said.

"Very well," James grumbled as he fished his keys out of his pocket. "But we were having such fun."

"We can keep having fun at the house," I said. "You pack up the leftover food and wine. We'll meet you at the car." I dragged Helen away.

"What's the matter with you?" she asked. "We were having fun."

"I've seen something that makes me think Taylor and Marcus are involved in Blake's death."

Helen blinked rapidly. "What did you see?"

"Taylor and her dog, Brutus. I think Taylor trained Dillon to push Blake overboard. I watched her own dog jump on her and shove her when Marcus performed a specific hand gesture."

"That's terrible," Helen said. "We should get her to explain herself." She made a move away from me, but I grabbed her arm.

"We need proof first," I said, "a way to get Taylor at the house and show everyone what she did."

"And why she did it," Helen said. "And how is Marcus involved?"

"It could be they're working together. He could be the one skimming the money out of the business. He didn't want me to study the accounts. It makes sense now if he's stealing. He got greedy and wanted more. Maybe Blake found out, or Marcus felt he needed him out of the way to avoid detection."

"Marcus is ambitious," Helen said. "He said he wanted to model himself on Blake and be the next big entrepreneur."

"We have to get them to confess to what they've done."

"Poor Dillon," Helen said. "Trained to kill his owner. It's so sad."

"We can be sad later," I said. "We've got to get the killers to confess to what they've done and make sure Honey isn't charged with a crime she didn't commit."

I drove us back to the house, my thoughts racing. James fell asleep on the back seat almost instantly, alongside Flipper, leaving Helen and me to talk.

"How about a dinner?" Helen suggested. "We could get everyone together to celebrate the arrival of Charlie. That way, it wouldn't seem weird if we invite Taylor.

You can get her to do tricks with Flipper and see if she reveals what she's done."

"That could work," I said. "But we need Julianne to witness it, and she's not even here."

"I'll be in charge of the dinner. I need a day or two to get everything together, so we don't have to do it tonight. We also need to make sure everyone is free to attend."

"We'll have it this Friday," I said. "Julianne will be back by then, and I'll message Taylor and ask her to come over."

"What about Marcus? How are you going to prove his involvement?"

"I'm still working on that," I said. "I need a direct link to what he's up to. If he's taking the money, there will be a trail, paper or electronic records that show he's stealing. We just need to find it."

"We need to do snooping *and* some cooking," Helen said as she rubbed her hands together. "My two favorite things."

I woke James up once we got back to the house and he staggered out of the car, running his hands through his hair as he did so. "Time for more wine?"

"We'll have to postpone the wine tasting," I said.

"That's such a pity. Are you sure I can't tempt you both?" James gave us a drunken smile.

"Another time," I said.

"Thanks for today, though," Helen said. "The wine was lovely."

He gave us a cheery wave before staggering off into the house. Hopefully, he'd sleep off his liquid lunch.

"What now?" Helen's eyes gleamed with excitement.

"We check out Marcus's room," I said. "He told me he has a room on the top floor. Let's find out what he's doing with the vineyard's money. And now's the perfect time. He's still out with Taylor."

Hurrying into the house, we dashed up the stairs to the top floor. After checking several rooms and finding a bathroom, storage room, and guest room, we came to the final door.

I did a quick check along the corridor, but there was no one around, so I eased open the door and looked inside.

The double bed was immaculately made, not a wrinkle on the sheets. The pillows looked brand-new. The dressing table had a neat row of men's toiletries on one side, looking like they'd been lined up using a ruler.

"This has to be his room." We hurried in, and I shut the door behind us, stationing Flipper by it to alert us if anyone came up the stairs.

"This place is like a showroom," Helen whispered. "Are you sure Marcus is human? I've never seen a man leave the bedroom so tidy."

I looked at the neatly arranged black slippers by the end of the bed. "He's a neat freak."

"Even I'm finding this level of neatness creepy," Helen said. "And I like everything tidy."

I had a quick look around the room. There was a desk in one corner and a filing cabinet next to it. That was the perfect place to start. "You check his dresser. I'll look over here."

"I'm afraid to touch anything," Helen said. "I bet he dusts for fingerprints every night. We'll have to make sure we don't leave incriminating evidence. If he finds one of my blonde hairs in here, I'll get in trouble."

"You won't have to worry about that for long if he's involved in Blake's death and stealing his money," I said as I opened the filing cabinet. "He'll be behind bars before he can tell you off for shedding hair."

Inside the filing cabinet were neatly labeled files from A to Z. I had to admit, I admired his system as I pulled out the banking file and skimmed through it. Everything was in date order in its own separate plastic folder. Looking through the paperwork, I couldn't spot anything incriminating, no strange sums of money going into his personal account. I checked a few more files, but there was nothing.

I placed the files back, making sure everything was lined up before closing the cabinet. I turned and looked at Helen. "Have you got anything useful over there?"

"I can't find anything," Helen said. "It looks like Marcus irons his pants, though."

"You're not supposed to be looking at his underwear," I said. "If he catches you, he'll think you're a pervert."

"Any man who irons his Y-fronts has got suspicious stamped all over him. Who has the time to do that? Even I don't iron my knickers!"

"Your standards are slipping."

"My standards are perfect," Helen said. "Ironed Y-fronts are not normal. Marcus has to be guilty."

I jumped as Flipper whined. Dillon had appeared next to him, his tongue hanging out, seeming pleased at having discovered us.

"Now's not a good time, Dillon," I said. "You don't want to distract Flipper. He's acting as our guard."

"We've got company?" Helen asked. "Is Blake here, as well?"

"No. Just Dillon."

"If he's still around, it suggests Blake might be too," Helen said. "And since they're still here, they must think Honey isn't involved in their deaths."

"Or Dillon is a confused ghost dog," I said. "I don't know if he even realizes he's even dead."

Flipper pawed at the ground and turned in a circle, his miserable gaze on Dillon.

"We need to hurry," I said. "I don't want Flipper getting sick in here. That would be impossible to cover up."

"I'll check the closet," Helen said. "You look in the chest of drawers."

We spent a couple of fruitless minutes hunting through Marcus's tidy drawers, coming out empty-handed.

Flipper whined again. We were out of time. "Maybe he keeps nothing in here. It might be too risky for him to have evidence in the house in case someone finds it and realizes what he's doing."

"Lack of evidence doesn't mean he's innocent, though," Helen said.

Flipper gave another whine before running away from Dillon and leaping onto Marcus's bed.

"Get down from there!" I said. "If you crumple the sheets, we'll get rumbled."

Flipper turned in a circle before laying on the duvet and giving me a sad-eyed stare.

"You can sleep in your own bed once we've finished searching."

Dillon raced across the room and joined Flipper on the bed, bouncing up and down beside him.

"That's not helping," I said. I hurried over to Flipper and caught hold of his collar. "Come on, boy. Let's get you out of here."

As Flipper reluctantly shuffled to the edge of the bed, I heard the faint sound of rustling paper.

I let go of Flipper and bent down.

"What are you looking at?" Helen hurried around the bed and joined me.

"I'm not certain." I eased my hand under the mattress and felt along the base. My fingers brushed some paper, and my heartrate increased. "I have a feeling Marcus is old school when it comes to hiding evidence."

"There's something under the mattress?" Helen ducked down and peered under it. "It had better not be smutty magazines."

I pulled out several sheets of paper, my eyes widening when I saw the financial transactions on them. I looked through the details of the money going into a Swiss bank account in the name of J.M. Smithe. "This is it! This is what we need to show that Marcus is stealing from the company. He set up an account in a false name and is filtering business funds into it."

"He killed Blake to avoid being discovered?" Helen asked.

"That must be it," I said.

"Now we know his motive, what about Taylor?"

I tapped my fingers on my chin. "I'm not sure. But at least we've got Marcus. He might talk when he realizes we're onto him."

"And we've got what we need to show Honey wasn't involved."

I nodded. "Your dinner will get everyone together. We can find out what's going on between Marcus and Taylor and prove to everyone that Honey is innocent."

Chapter 22

"A dinner sounds lovely," Julianne said. "It'll be a fun way to welcome Charlie to the household."

"I'm always up for a party," James said, who lounged on the sofa by the window in Julianne's office, supposedly reading the latest business plan she'd put together.

It was the evening after our discovery of the J.M. Smithe paperwork, and our plan to reveal the real killers was underway.

"I was thinking Friday night," I said. "Helen's an excellent cook and has agreed to do the food for us."

"And we should have it on the yacht," James said.

I grinned at him. It was as if he'd read my mind.

Julianne's smile faded. "Must we?"

I put on my best sympathetic face. "From what I hear, Blake spent some of his happiest days on that yacht."

"He'd think it was a hoot we were welcoming a new dog into the family on there," James said. "He'd want the party on the Orwell."

Julianne pulled her shoulders back. "You're right. It's no good dwelling on the bad things that happened there. Let's have the dinner. And I look forward to Helen's cooking."

"And the wine," James said. "I'll organize that."

"I should hope so," Julianne said dryly, "considering you're part owner of the vineyard."

James chortled. "Always a pleasure to serve."

"Shall we say seven o'clock?" I suggested. "And since we're celebrating Charlie's arrival, I thought we could invite Taylor as well."

"That's a great idea," Julianne said. "She always has fun stories about training her animals. And she'll be a big part of Charlie's life, so it's only right she's there."

Everything was almost in place. I left Julianne and James to discuss business and hurried to the kitchen to find Helen beginning preparations for our evening meal. "You need to get out your cookbooks."

"Did Julianne agree to the dinner party?" Helen's eyes brightened.

"She did."

Helen let out a squeak. "There are so many recipes I want to try."

I dug out the card Taylor gave me and sent her a message inviting her to the dinner. "We need to make sure our dog training suspect can come."

"What if she refuses?" Helen's smile slipped. "She could feel weird about going back to the scene of the crime."

"It would be stranger if she didn't turn up. She needs to act like everything is normal." My phone pinged and I grinned as I checked the message. "Taylor would love to come."

Helen clapped her hands together. "It's time for me to create a fabulous dinner."

"And time for us to catch the killers."

I couldn't hide my nerves as I made my way to the yacht. It was the evening of the dinner and everyone would be there. Marcus, Taylor, Channing, James, and Julianne, along with Helen and me.

I'd done nothing like this before. It felt very Miss Marple, bringing everyone together to do a big reveal. I was out of my depth. What if I was making a mistake? What if this had been an accident and I was making up the whole thing? J.M. Smithe could be a legitimate business. Blake might even have asked Marcus to set it up, and he was only following his late boss's orders. Taylor might not have trained Dillon to kill Blake and had simply been showing Marcus a neat doggy trick. If that was true, I'd lose my job and get a terrible reference. It would ruin my career.

But the evidence from the accounts was convincing. Marcus had been stealing from the company. Perhaps Taylor had discovered what he was up to and insisted on getting a cut. Whatever had gone on, tonight would reveal it all. Or I would end up looking very foolish.

I climbed on board the Orwell and headed below deck, the tempting smells of tarragon, parsley, butter, and skate drawing me to the kitchen.

Helen was in full-on cooking mode, with a white apron tied around her middle and her hair pulled off her face with a black headscarf. Several pots sat on the stove and the oven belted out heat.

"Is there anything I can help with?" I asked.

"Don't you come near any of this." Helen glared at me. "I've tried your cooking. We don't want you to jinx tonight's meal."

"How's the sea sickness?"

"You know, I've not thought about it. Maybe keeping busy is the answer. I've been so distracted by the food that I haven't noticed the sway of the boat under my feet." Her cheeks grew pale. "Until you just mentioned it."

I grinned at her. "I'll go set the table."

"Yes. Keep out of here until everything is ready. Then you can help me to serve."

I gathered up the cutlery. "Everyone will be here in the next twenty minutes."

Helen squeaked. "There's still so much to do."

"It smells amazing. Everyone will love your food. And that's not the thing we need to be worried about. I'm about to uncover two killers to our boss."

"It's the thing *I* need to worry about," Helen said. "You're the one who'll do the fabulous revelation about Blake's murder."

My stomach roiled at the thought. "This wasn't such a great idea."

Helen slowed her manic whisking. "Are you worried?"

I nodded. "What if Julianne doesn't believe me?"

"Why wouldn't she? Marcus and Taylor did this. We both saw the paperwork showing Marcus is stealing from the business. And you saw Taylor teaching doggy tricks that could have ended in murder. What does your gut tell you?"

I glanced around the kitchen. "That at least the food will be amazing."

Helen flapped a dishcloth at me. "Get out of here before I make a mistake. Go make the table look lovely and wait for everyone to arrive. This evening will be perfect for everyone, apart from Marcus and Taylor. And they deserve it."

"Yes, boss." I left her to her final preparations and walked to the top deck where we had arranged a table. I laid it with a white linen tablecloth, matching plates, and shining silver cutlery. I was just setting the glasses when James strolled up the steps, carrying several bottles of wine.

He grinned when he saw me. "I thought you might like to get these chilled before everyone arrives."

I grabbed two bottles from his hands. "Thanks. This will go perfectly with the fish."

"Fish, again!" James said. "Anyone would think we live by the sea."

"Too true." My laugh sounded too loud and fake and my hands shook as I set the bottles down.

"Is everything okay?" James asked. "You seem a little on edge."

"I'm fine. I just want to make sure tonight goes well."

"Don't get anxious about a party for a puppy. The poor thing won't have a clue what's going on."

"I hope he does. Helen's even made him his own dog friendly cake. I hate to think what's inside, but make sure to avoid the cake with the dog paw iced on the top."

"Good tip. The party will be just perfect." James glanced around the deck. "Shall I get the wine open?"

I nodded and took a calming breath as I looked out over the marina. The water was still and the sun was lowering toward the horizon. We had a good hour until dusk, and there were lights dotted around the deck, so we could stay out until it got too cold. That gave me plenty of time to reveal my theory about Taylor and Marcus.

"And you're sure everything is okay?" James uncorked a bottle of wine and poured two glasses.

"Everything is perfect," I said. "Why do you ask?"

"Oh, nothing." James glanced down at my hands.

I realized I was gripping the railings so hard my knuckles were white. I let go and shook out my fingers. "I'll take that glass of wine if it's for me."

"Of course. The perfect way to loosen up." He handed me a glass, and I took a large sip.

Flipper jumped to his feet and stared behind James. Blake and Dillon popped into view and hovered by the steps.

James shivered. "I hope this breeze doesn't get any worse. We might have to take things below deck if it does."

I discreetly gestured to Dillon and Blake to move away from James, but I was glad they were there. Blake needed to see how Taylor and Marcus reacted to my accusations, and I wanted to know what his thoughts were on their involvement in his death.

"I can see the others," James said, pointing toward the marina car park.

I turned and saw Julianne and Marcus leading the way, Channing behind them. They boarded the yacht and we greeted each other while James did an excellent job of making sure everyone had plenty to drink.

Helen rushed up the steps with a tray of hors d'oeuvres and thrust them into my hand. "Pass these around. The first course will be ready in ten minutes."

I did as I was told, keeping an eye on Dillon and Blake to make sure they behaved themselves. They seemed content watching people mingle and chat.

Julianne had Charlie in her arms, a smart red collar around his neck. He squirmed as he spotted Flipper and barked, trying to get free so they could play.

Flipper narrowed his eyes and tucked his tail away. It looked like he wasn't keen on having his tail used as a plaything again. Can't say I blamed him.

"I'm not letting this one go," Julianne said, as I stopped in front of her with the tray of hors d'oeuvres. "He's so tiny, he'll slip straight through the railings." Her gaze shifted to the side of the yacht. "And I can't bear to think of losing him in that way."

Channing patted her arm. "We're here to celebrate Charlie's inclusion in our family. It's a time to be happy."

Julianne's chin wobbled, but she nodded. Her gaze appeared to rest on the exact spot Dillon and Blake were standing. "Hopefully, they're looking down on us, watching us have a nice time."

"I'm sure they are." I turned as I heard running feet, and was relieved to see Taylor climbing onto the yacht, Brutus at her heel.

"I hope I'm not too late," she said. "One of the dogs escaped. I had to get him back before I could leave." She brushed a piece of fur off her black pants. "I didn't even have time to change. Dog fur gets on everything."

"You look great," I said to her. "And thanks for coming. I know it was last minute, but it wouldn't have been right you not being here, given we're celebrating Charlie." I offered her some hors d'oeuvres and tried to sound as friendly as possible, while all the time, the word *murderer* kept skating through my thoughts.

She grabbed several pastries from the tray. "These smell lovely. And I'm starving. No time for lunch today, but I wanted to save my appetite for tonight."

Helen emerged from below deck, her hair now neatly curled and her lipstick immaculate. Only Helen could pull off a three-course meal for half a dozen people and come out looking like she's just spent the day in the spa. "If everyone would like to take their seats, the first course will be served shortly." She cast me a meaningful look. I guessed it meant I was helping serve.

I hurried below deck with the almost empty tray of hors d'oeuvres. "Everyone is here."

"How you feeling now?" she asked.

"Terrified I'm about to make a mistake," I said. "What if this doesn't work?"

"You'll be apologizing to Taylor and Marcus for the short time you're employed here."

"That's not comforting."

Helen handed me two plates with dressed salad and olives. "You know what you saw. You're convinced this is what happened, and you want to make sure the right thing is done by Blake and Dillon. And we need to get Honey free."

"I do. And you're right. Honey is still in police custody, and that's wrong." I wished I was as confident as Helen sounded.

"So, you need to find out if your theory is right," Helen said. "If it all goes wrong, blame the booze. That's always a good way to get out of any mess up."

I squared my shoulders and headed back up to the deck. I had to do this. There was no backing out now.

Once was seated and the first course eaten. Helen disappeared to put the finishing touches to the main course. I'd made sure I was sitting next to Taylor, who was sandwiched between Marcus and me.

"What sort of tricks can you teach the dogs?" I asked Taylor.

"Anything you want."

"Could you get Flipper to do tricks?"

"If you wanted him to," Taylor said, glancing over at Flipper, who was suspiciously sniffing an olive that had fallen off someone's plate. "What sort of training does he have?"

"He's a free-spirited dog." I needed to maintain his cover. "But as an assistance dog, he can do all sorts of useful things. He mainly alerts me when I'm unwell."

"That's a handy skill to have," Taylor said. "I've done training with assistance dogs in the past. Taught them to get clean washing out of the machine, that sort of thing."

"Show me some of the things Brutus can do," I said.

Taylor looked around the table. "Now isn't the right time."

"Come on," James said from across the table. "We need entertainment in-between courses."

"Oh, yes, do," Julianne said. "Give me an idea of what I'll be able to teach Charlie."

Taylor patted her pockets and pulled out a few doggy treats. "A couple of tricks won't hurt." She stood from her seat and gestured to Brutus. He instantly rolled over.

Everyone clapped politely, and Charlie barked.

"You want to have a go at that, Flipper?" I asked him.

He covered his paw with his nose, and everyone laughed.

"Can you make Brutus jump up?" I asked.

Taylor's eyebrows quirked. "I don't encourage dogs to jump on people. It's not popular."

"I don't want Charlie to learn how to jump up," Julianne said. "Make sure you don't teach him that."

"I won't," Taylor said. "He'll learn the usual obedience tricks when he's old enough."

"What if you wanted a dog to push someone?" I asked, watching Taylor's reaction carefully. "Could you train a dog to do that?"

"Push an object you mean?"

I looked over to where Blake was hovering by the edge of the yacht. I stood and walked over to stand next to him. "No. An actual person. Could you get a dog to push me?"

"You wouldn't want that to happen," Channing said. "You might go overboard."

A hush descended around the table. Everyone stared at me.

I kept my attention on Taylor and saw her face pale.

"Would you be able to get a dog to do that?" I persisted.

Taylor gripped the back of her seat. "What exactly are you asking me?"

Marcus grabbed hold of her hand, but she shook him away.

"Isn't it strange how Blake fell overboard and Dillon went with him," I said, casting an eye around the group to see I had everyone's attention.

"It was a horrible accident," Taylor said.

"And didn't you tell me you taught Dillon obedience tricks once a week in private lessons while he was alive?"

"I did," Taylor said slowly. "It was the arrangement I had with the family. Free use of the training field in return for helping out with Dillon."

"What's this all about?" Julianne asked.

I ignored her question. "So you got the chance to teach Dillon new tricks?"

"I could if I wanted to," Taylor said cautiously. She flashed a nervous glance at Marcus. "But I didn't."

"You didn't teach Dillon to jump up and push Blake overboard?" I asked.

A horrified silence was replaced by a jumble of voices as people yelled questions at Taylor and me.

"What's she talking about?" Julianne looked at Taylor.

"This is nonsense," Marcus spluttered. "Blake's death was an accident."

"Do you really think that's what happened?" James looked around the table in surprise, his glass of wine dangling from his hand.

"Quiet!" Julianne jumped to her feet and slammed her hand on the table. "Lorna, are you being serious? Do you think Taylor trained Dillon to hurt Blake?"

I swallowed my nerves. "I do."

"This is ridiculous," Taylor said. "Why would I do that? I liked Blake. He was a decent guy. I get no benefit from him being dead."

"You would if you were working with Marcus," I said.

Marcus spluttered out a few more nonsense words before jumping to his feet. "What are you talking about?" He looked over at Julianne. "The woman is deranged."

Julianne raised a hand. "I want to hear her out. Lorna, tell me what you know. What has Marcus been doing?"

"He's stealing from the business," I said.

More spluttering came from Marcus. "I've never stolen so much as a paperclip."

"Maybe you haven't," I said. "But your false business name, J.M. Smithe, is getting rich from the money you're skimming."

Marcus's jaw dropped. "How do you know about that?"

"Shut up, idiot," Taylor hissed. She glared at me. "You've got no proof of any of this."

"I saw you training your own dog. You've taught Brutus how to jump up and push people. It wouldn't have been difficult for you to do the same with Dillon and make sure he had a trigger, so he shoved Blake overboard when prompted."

"I didn't do that," Taylor said. "And you can't prove I did."

"Don't you use a dog whistle in your training?"

Taylor folded her arms over her chest. "What if I do?"

"Mind if I use it?"

"You're not having my dog whistle."

"For goodness sake! Give her the whistle and let's sort this out," Julianne said. "If Lorna has made a mistake, you have nothing to hide."

Taylor grudgingly thrust the dog whistle at me. "Now what?"

"Marcus, come and stand next to me."

Marcus blinked rapidly. "Why should I?"

"I have a theory that needs testing," I said.

"Can't somebody else test the theory?"

"It should really be you," I said. "If you're as involved in Blake and Dillon's deaths as I think you are, it's only fair you re-enact their last moment together."

I heard Marcus swallow, even though he was still standing by the table. "I'm not sure about this."

"Stand next to Lorna," Julianne snapped. "If you want to keep your job, you'll do this."

Marcus hung his head and stomped toward me. He shot me an evil glare. "You don't know what you're doing. You're making a big mistake."

"I don't think so," I said. "And I think you know what's about to happen, as well. Make sure you take a deep breath."

He shot me a panicked look as I lifted the dog whistle to my lips. "Wait! I can cut you in."

"Marcus! Shut up." Taylor took a step closer.

He grabbed my arm. "I can pay you more than Julianne does. Whatever you want."

I raised my eyebrows. "I'm not interested in a bribe."

"Marcus!" Julianne's tone made my blood chill. "Stand by the edge of the yacht and don't you dare move."

I shot her a grateful look as Marcus grumbled under his breath, but he let go of my arm.

"I need to remember what your hand gestures were to make Brutus jump up." I took a second to compose myself. "You make a fist, spin it in the air anticlockwise, and then shove it forward."

Marcus grabbed hold of the railing as I made the gesture and then blew into the whistle.

"Wait!" Taylor yelled.

It was too late. Brutus and Dillon's ears pricked up. They shot straight at Marcus, smashing into him at the same time. Dillon passed right through him, but Brutus almost head-butted Marcus as they flew straight over the railings.

"Brutus!" Taylor raced to the side of the yacht and dove over without hesitation.

"What about me?" Marcus yelled. He clung to the side for half a second, before his fingers slipped from the railing and he plunged into the water.

Everyone was on their feet, racing to the side of the yacht and staring down at Marcus, Brutus, and Taylor.

Taylor had hold of Brutus and was swimming toward the jetty. Marcus was left to splash around on his own.

"Is it true?" Julianne turned her wide eyes to me. "Marcus and Taylor killed Blake?"

"It is," I said. "I saw them training with Brutus and suddenly realized how easy it would be to get a dog to push Blake off the yacht."

Julianne gaped at me. "And the money?"

"Marcus has been stealing from you for a long time. I've got paperwork to show where it is. And I think Taylor found out about it and they've been working together ever since."

"That scheming little snot," Julianne said as she glared down into the water.

"Someone help me!" Marcus flailed around.

Flipper ambled over and sat at my feet, looking up at me and letting his tongue hang out.

"There's no need to save Marcus," I said to him. "He got himself into this mess."

"The only help he'll get is from the police." Julianne was already pulling out her phone, Charlie still tucked into the crook of her elbow.

Flipper's gaze shifted to Helen, who staggered up the steps with a tray of skate and perfectly roasted vegetables. She stared at the chaos on deck with a frown on her face before looking at the food and sighing.

I listened to Julianne tell the police what was going on and watched as Channing threw a float to Marcus. Taylor was now flopped on the jetty, her arms around Brutus.

A cold touch fell on my shoulder and I turned to see Blake. Dillon was by his side. I moved away from the chaos so I could speak to him without being overheard.

"Is everything okay with you?" I asked softly.

Blake nodded. He looked over his shoulder and shook his head at the scene behind him.

"I guess this is all a shock. But now you know what happened the night you went overboard. Honey had nothing to do with this. Your daughter is innocent."

He nodded again and then petted Dillon's head. He wasn't blaming his dog for any of this, and for that, I was glad. As Taylor had said, you can teach a dog to do just about anything when you offer them their favorite treat, even how to kill their owner.

"Is it time to move on?" I asked him.

Blake touched my arm, gave me a smile, and they both vanished.

Chapter 23

It had been a week since the revelations at the dinner on board the Orwell. Everything felt like it was returning to normal. Well, as normal as it could after something like that.

Marcus and Taylor had been arrested for murder, Honey had been released, and Blake and Dillon were gone.

I walked along the hallway toward Julianne's office with an armful of folders, Flipper by my side. I paused as I heard someone talking softly.

Honey was curled on the sofa in the garden room, her feet tucked underneath her and a large mug in her hands. Her gaze was on the garden outside. Much to my surprise, sitting snuggled next to her was a tiny brown puppy, his nose tucked under his tail and his eyes tightly shut.

"How's everything going?" I asked as I walked into the room.

Honey turned and smiled at me. "I still feeling weird about how everything has turned out. I can't quite believe this is all mine. And I have you to thank for that." She looked around the room and shook her head.

And it was all hers. The caveat in Blake's will meant that Honey now owned the family home. "Do you know what you'll do with the place?"

Her nose wrinkled. "It's too big for me to live in on my own. I was thinking I might sell it, maybe go cruising on Dad's yacht. It'll give me a chance to clear my head and figure out what I actually want to do with the rest of my life. I've got lots to think about."

"Is that little guy coming with you?" I looked down at the sleeping puppy.

"He is." Honey grinned. "I was being silly feeling scared of dogs. It's time to have someone loyal by my side. And there's nothing more loyal than a dog. I've named him Blake Junior."

The puppy opened one sleepy eye, gave a large yawn, and curled into a ball again.

"You can't beat a dog for loyalty," I said. "He's just what you need."

"I've been thinking about Blake's remaining family," Honey said. "Julianne still has the business and Channing has apologized for the fight we had. He is my uncle, so I'll give him a second chance, and he's already given back the watch he took and the car. He's trying to make amends."

"If you decide to keep the house, you can offer him a place here."

"Maybe," Honey said. "I always thought he didn't have much direction. I was just the same until I met my dad. I was never sure what I wanted to do with my life. But seeing him with so much passion and drive helped give me focus. That's what Channing needs as well. Working for things, instead of just taking them, will do him good."

"Do you mind me asking about Julianne? Since this is now your house, you can make her leave."

"The thought has crossed my mind." Honey gave me a wry smile. "But I get why she behaved the way she did. She thought I was having an affair with her husband. I'd have been just as mean. Maybe even meaner."

The sound of nails scraping across the wooden floor boards had me turning. Charlie raced around the corner, skidding as he did so, before he launched himself at Blake Junior.

"Come back, you naughty boy!" Julianne shot around the corner and froze as she saw us. "Oh! I didn't realize you were in here. I'll leave."

Charlie bounced around Blake Junior, who opened his eyes and stared at him, before rolling off the sofa. They both tumbled to the floor in a mess of puppy limbs and flapping ears.

Julianne ran forward, her hands outstretched as she attempted to separate the dogs. "I've no idea how to train him. I always relied on Taylor to do that sort of thing." She caught hold of Charlie and scooped him into her arms.

"I'm not sure what to do with Blake Junior either," Honey said quietly.

The two women stared at each other in silence.

"I am sorry," Julianne said, "for everything."

Honey let out a sigh. "I didn't mean to cause you any problems. I just wanted to find my family."

Julianne placed a hand on Honey's knee. "And you have. I know we're not related by blood, and I'll understand if you want nothing to do with me, but I'd like you to be a part of this family."

I sucked in a breath, half-expecting Honey to tell her where to stick her offer. I wouldn't blame her if she did after everything Julianne had put her through.

Honey's eyes sparkled and she smiled. "I'd love that. I just wish Blake was still around to be a part of it. I would like to get to know everyone better."

"I'd love that, too." Julianne sat next to Honey. "I have a stepdaughter!"

"I think time away would do us all some good, though," Honey said. "I need to go see my mom for a few days, and make sure she's doing okay. Maybe even invite her to stay here sometime if that's not a problem for you."

"No! Your mother is most welcome." Julianne chewed on her bottom lip. "I mean, it might be a little awkward, but she must come. We'll work something out."

"Maybe time by the sea will do her good," Honey said. "There's an excellent cancer unit at the local hospital. She'll get the best of care. And I was just saying to Lorna that I might take Dad's yacht out, do some sailing. Although, I'll need a few lessons on how to sail before I go out on my own. There are a lot of things new for us, a lot of things we all need to figure out."

"Blake would like you to do that," Julianne said. "I know he loved you, and he adored being on the water. I think that's a perfect idea."

Honey nodded. "And I'm not in any hurry to do anything with this house. You're welcome to stay if you want to, and help me work out what to do with the place."

Julianne smiled and glanced around the room. "This house does have a lot of memories. Not all of them good. It might be time for me to move on as well. Find a place of my own, somewhere smaller for Charlie and me to enjoy."

"You're not going to leave the village?" Honey asked.

"No, the village is where I belong," Julianne said. "And I need to be close by to keep an eye on the vineyard. But like you said, we've all got time to think things through and figure out what we really want."

They shared a smile.

"If you need anyone to take care of Blake Junior while you're away, I know someone who'll be very happy to have him as a playmate." Julianne placed Charlie on the floor.

The two puppies began chasing each other and rolling around again.

We all watched the puppies dance around, Flipper keeping out of the way and making warning grumbles every time they got too close to him, his tail tucked firmly between his paws.

Julianne looked over at me. "Thank you for everything you've done for this family. I guess it's a shock coming into a new job and discovering a murderer in your midst."

I suppressed a grin. It was more common than she realized. "I was happy to help."

"That's good to hear," Julianne said. "When I saw your young man arrive outside a few minutes ago, I thought he might be here to take you away from all the drama."

My heartbeat sped up. "Zach's here?"

"Didn't you know he was coming?" Julianne asked. "I spoke to him for several minutes. Such a charming man. I can see why you're so smitten by him."

A surprise visit from Zach. I grinned, already turning to the door. "I'll leave you both to it." I put down the folders I was carrying and hurried to the front door.

Zach was waiting outside by his Land Rover. He had his phone in his hand and looked up in surprise as he saw me.

"I was just about to text you."

"What are you doing here?" I ran over to him, Jessie already springing to her paws and barking with pleasure as she saw Flipper.

"I hated how we left things." Zach caught me in his arms. "I know we said sorry on the phone, but I was still feeling bad."

"Me too. I'm sorry for blaming you for my missing things."

"No! I'm the one who needs to be sorry." Zach ducked his head. "It definitely wasn't you."

"Did you find out it was Gunner messing around?"

"No. It wasn't him either. And he's here as well. He made a lame excuse about wanting to get in some surfing, but we all know the real reason he's here." Zach grinned at me.

"So, if Gunner wasn't moving our stuff, then what's going on?" I tilted my head to one side.

"I've got a confession to make. There's something I've not been telling you."

I clenched my teeth. I knew what this was about. "Actually, so have I."

Zach looked surprised. "What's your confession?"

I took a deep breath. "I accidentally found the ring box."

He looked confused. "What ring are you talking about?"

"The engagement ring you've got hidden in your sock drawer. It is for me, isn't it?"

Zach scrubbed a hand across his face. "No. That's not your ring."

My stomach dropped. "You're going to ask somebody else to marry you?"

He let out a sigh. "Not for a second. That ring doesn't belong to you. Actually, it's part of what I need to tell you about. That ring belonged to my wife."

I stared open-mouthed at Zach. My heart thudded so hard in my chest it made me dizzy.

Jessie and Flipper raced around the side of the house, giving happy little barks, but I barely heard them as I gaped at Zach. A thousand questions formed in my head, but no words came out.

Helen and Gunner emerged from the house, and despite my heart shattering shock, I mentally stored away the fact they were holding hands. But all I could focus on was the fact Zach had just told me he had a wife. He was dating me, living with me, and he was already married.

"Are you enjoying your time by the sea?" Gunner asked. "It sure is beautiful around here."

I flapped my hand at him, finally able to speak, but my gaze was glued to Zach as I backed away from him. "You're married! That's your wife's ring in your sock drawer?"

"What's going on?" Helen dropped her hold on Gunner's hand and stalking toward us.

Gunner hurried forward and wrapped an arm around her waist before she got too near. "Now might be a good time for you to show me the garden."

"Forget the garden," Helen said. "Lorna, are you okay?"

I shook my head, tears in my eyes. "No!"

"Let me explain," Zach said, his anxious gaze shooting from Helen to me. "My wife is dead. And I think... I think she's haunting our house."

My mouth fell open again, while Helen made a series of spluttering noises.

"You have a dead wife?" I forced out. "Your wife's ghost is in our home?"

Helen glared at Gunner. "Did you know about this?"

He rubbed the back of his neck. "Erm, Zach's mentioned it."

"I mean, about the wife?" Helen glared at him. "You knew Zach was married?"

"Oh! Well, sure. I was at the wedding."

She thumped him in the arm. "And you never told me."

"It's not my news to tell." Gunner rubbed his arm. "How about that trip around the garden now?"

"I'm not leaving Lorna at a time like this," Helen said.

I shook myself out of the shock I felt. "Go. I need to speak to Zach alone."

"Only if you're sure," Helen said.

I nodded at her. "I'll be fine." Well, I hoped I'd be fine. I'd just found out my boyfriend had a wife, and she was dead. *And* she was haunting him. I grabbed hold of Zach's arm and pulled him away so we could talk alone. "You've been married before?"

"I was very young when we got married. I realized straight away it was a mistake."

"Why didn't you tell me?"

"Would it have made a difference to us?"

"I'm not sure. Maybe. Why keep something like that from me?"

"Because it was a long time ago and a part of my past I'm not proud about," Zach said. "I left her after she cheated on me. But I was glad it happened, glad I had a reason to get out."

I ran my hands through my hair. "Tell me about her."

Zach shrugged. "There's nothing to tell. She hasn't been in my life for a long time."

"What's her name?"

"Amelia."

I instantly hated that name, despite how pretty it was. "How old were you when you got married?"

"Eighteen," Zach said. "We met at college. She was the one pushing for marriage, and I liked her, so I agreed. We got married in the local registry office and moved in together. It all happened within a year of us meeting. I got caught up in the excitement. Then reality hit and it wasn't so much fun."

"So you abandoned her?"

"No! I stuck it out for three years. And she cheated on me! I was focused on getting my qualifications and not interested in parties and getting wasted every night. She said I was boring and found someone else."

I let out a breath, a little of my shock and anger fading. "Eighteen is young to do something so grown-up." I thought back to when I was eighteen. I still had posters of boy bands inside my closet and secretly dreamed of a hunk on a motorbike arriving and whisking me away for an adventure. I couldn't imagine getting married at such a young age, even if my leather clad biker hunk had asked me to become Mrs. Motorbike Hottie.

"And people change," Zach said. "I've changed a lot since I was that age."

"They do." My anger continued to lessen, but he wasn't forgiven yet. "Why do you think Amelia is haunting our house?"

"I found out three months ago that she died in a car crash," Zach said. "I was sorry to hear the news. Although we parted on bad terms, I wouldn't wish that on her. It wasn't long after that, that I started having strange dreams."

"You've never mentioned them to me."

"I just thought it was my head messing with me," Zach looked away. "I started dreaming about Amelia."

My anger reared up again, but I fought against it. "She would be on your mind after you found out she was dead."

"It wasn't so much that," Zach said. "I read about her death in the paper and it surprised me. But I got images of her in my head when I was asleep. And when we moved into the house, I got shivers in certain rooms. Then things started to go missing. That's when I wondered, could it be Amelia? Could she be haunting me and trying to get my attention?"

I forced myself to keep calm and remain as analytical as possible, despite feeling jealous of a ghost. "Why would she do that?"

"You always say ghosts stay around because they have unfinished business," Zach said. "And I have unfinished business with her. We never got divorced. Until she died, we were technically married. Maybe that's why she's come back."

An unpleasant thought entered my head. "You were going to propose to me while still being married to Amelia?"

"No! But when I found out she'd died, I felt as if I was free to marry again."

"And you *were* thinking of asking me to marry you?" My pulse fluttered at the idea. I was still angry with Zach for keeping this secret, but I sort of understood why he'd done it.

"It's been on my mind," Zach said, giving me a wry smile. "But that ring isn't for you. It was Amelia's. When I left her, she threw it at me. I found it when I was packing up my stuff and wanted to keep it somewhere so I wouldn't forget about it again. I was going to get rid of it. It doesn't have many happy memories attached to it."

"I'm glad to hear you weren't going to give me your dead wife's ring."

"No! That would be creepy," Zach said. "When I found out that Amelia had died, it gave me a nudge to get a move on and ask before someone else snapped you up."

I shook my head. That was never likely to happen. "You know I'm with you. You have nothing to worry about."

He gave me a cautious smile. "I messed up. I should have been up front with you about Amelia when we got together."

"Yes, you should. But I sort of understand. It sounds like you weren't happy."

"You still had a right to know."

"I haven't told you about all my previous boyfriends."

Zach's brows lowered. "Have there been many?"

"No one important. No one like you. I would have liked to have been told about Amelia. I would also have liked to have known you were married. It feels strange us being together and you having a wife."

"I am sorry about that. What do you think about her haunting our house, though?" Zach scratched his chin. "Am I being stupid?"

I chewed on my bottom lip. "The things going missing is strange, but I've not sensed a ghost in the house and neither has Flipper. Although, Jessie does keep him distracted."

"Maybe she only appears when I'm on my own," Zach said. "Can ghosts do that? Pick and choose when they drop in."

"They can," I said. "She could just be appearing when you're around. But if she's doing that, how can we communicate with her?"

"I have tried speaking to her," Zach said. "It doesn't make much difference. I still feel the cold spots and things are still going missing."

"Whatever's going on, we need to get it sorted," I said. I wasn't willing to share Zach with another woman, even if she was dead.

"So, you'll help me figure this out?"

I stepped closer. "Of course, I will. We're in this together. We help each other. Always." A big part of me wanted to scream and shout. It took every ounce of my grown-up self not to tell Zach what a moron he was. It wasn't right what he'd done, keeping this from me.

"I wondered if you might hate me."

"I'm not happy, but I don't hate you." I kissed his cheek, still keeping my sensible, grown-up side in charge. "And I understand. We'll figure out how to get Amelia to show herself and work out why she's haunting you and what we need to do to get her out."

"I knew your ghost skills would come in handy one day."

I glared at him. "My ghost skills come in handy all the time. You've just never needed them before. Now, you'll get to see my superpower in action."

"I can't wait." He kissed the top of my head.

"So, I guess this means I won't get a proposal from you soon?"

Zach hugged me to him. "You'll get one."

With all the conflicting thoughts in my head, I wasn't so sure we were ready for marriage. "Any chance you could tell me when? If we don't get married soon, Helen will go crazy. She's planned out the whole thing, from the cake to the dress."

"Helen needs to focus on her own relationship." Zach looked over my head, and I turned to see Gunner and Helen still holding hands as they walked around the garden.

She looked in my direction, and I gave her a thumbs up to show everything was okay. Well, it wasn't okay, it was all a bit of a mess. I was still not sure I'd forgiven Zach. Would I have done things differently in his position? I honestly didn't know.

"Their secret is out," I said.

"Not that they were any good at hiding it," Zach said. "How about we have a joint wedding? That could be fun."

I grimaced. "Helen's idea of a wedding is very different to mine. Unless you want over the top celebrations, a classical orchestra playing as I walk up the aisle, and a five-tiered cake, we'd better make our own plans."

"Whatever you want," Zach said. "Now, why don't you tell me what's been going on here? Have you figured out what happened on the yacht?"

He might have changed the subject, but I was still thinking things through. The Amelia subject wouldn't go away that easily. "It's all sorted. The ghosts are happy, the killers have been caught and the family is back together."

"Your superpowers have come good again."

"As always." As I tried to relax, my thoughts tangled together. I wasn't happy about Amelia being in our house, or about Zach keeping this from me.

As soon as I could, I'd return home and have a few words with Amelia. She had no claim over Zach, and I didn't share when it came to my boyfriends. I was the only woman in Zach's life, not counting Jessie. But doubt still niggled. He'd kept such a big thing from me. Was he hiding anything else I should know about?

I watched the dogs chase each other around the garden and Helen scold Gunner for saying something inappropriate. No. I had to believe Zach was as honest as I'd always thought him to be.

This was my own family, weird and wonderful as it was. It was just as it should be. No ghost from Zach's past was going to mess that up. Not ever.

***

Want to find out what's next for Lorna and Flipper? Get **Ghostly Play** and meet the new ghosts in Lorna's life.

Read on to learn more.

Ghostly Play

Death by armed drone. A ghost with a bad case of the blues. Some cute pigs looking for a friend.

Lorna Shadow, Helen, and Flipper arrive at their jobs with the newly made millionaire, Alex Hudson. Lorna quickly realizes she'll need to **play surrogate mother** as well as personal assistant to her young, brilliant, and confused new employer, who prefers playing war games on his computer rather than growing a business empire.

She can handle that. And there shouldn't be any ghosts lurking in their new state-of-the-art home. This job will be easy. It's a pity her hopes of a good old-fashioned bit of admin are shattered when the ghost of Alex's best friend, Greg, appears. And when the unusual manner of his death emerges – being shot in the back by an armed drone – Lorna's curiosity is raised.

And with the **ghost refusing to leave,** she begins her investigation. Was this a tragic accident or is there a murderer on the loose?

As Lorna learns more about the family and the

business, **dark motives** for murder emerge, and it becomes clear that a lot of people wanted Greg dead. And that's just wrong.

It's time for sleuthing, clue hunting, and finding the truth. But Lorna's struggling as she's torn between helping the ghost and tackling her complicated home life. If she fails, she could lose Zach, a killer will remain free, and an innocent man won't get the justice he deserves.

Enjoy this fun-filled **cozy ghost mystery**. Meet some cute pigs with a naughty streak and puzzle through the clues to discover the murderer.

Enjoy Ghostly Play in paperback or e-book.

About the Author

K.E. O'Connor (Karen) is the author of the adorably fun Lorna Shadow cozy ghost mystery series, the wickedly funny Crypt Witch paranormal mystery series, the Magical Misfits Mysteries featuring a sassy cat with a bundle of twisty puzzles to solve, the slightly darker Witch Haven paranormal mystery series featuring four troubled witches and their wonderful furry (feathered and web-slinging companions), and the whimsical, delicious Holly Holmes cozy culinary mysteries.

Stay in touch with the fun mysteries:

Newsletter: www.subscribepage.com/cozymysteries
Website: www.keoconnor.com
Facebook: www.facebook.com/keoconnorauthor

Complete series list

Ghostly Manners
Ghostly Secrets
Ghostly Games
Ghostly Affairs
Ghostly Business
Ghostly Rules
Ghostly Waves
Ghostly Play
Ghostly Proposal
Ghostly Vows
Ghostly Fright
Ghostly Hunt
Ghostly Surprises